THE LAND OF MYSTERY

EDWARD S. ELLIS

The Land of Mystery

Edward S. Ellis

© 1st World Library, 2007
PO Box 2211
Fairfield, IA 52556
www.1stworldlibrary.com
First Edition

LCCN: 2007927777

Softcover ISBN: 978-1-4218-4529-6
Hardcover ISBN: 978-1-4218-4445-9
eBook ISBN: 978-1-4218-4613-2

Purchase *"The Land of Mystery"*
as a traditional bound book at:
www.1stWorldLibrary.com/purchase.asp?ISBN=978-1-4218-4529-6

1ˢᵗ World Library Literary Society

Giving Back to the World

"If you want to work on the core problem, it's early school literacy."

- James Barksdale, former CEO of Netscape

"No skill is more crucial to the future of a child, or to a democratic and prosperous society, than literacy."

- Los Angeles Times

"Literacy... means far more than learning how to read and write... The aim is to transmit... knowledge and promote social participation."

- UNESCO

"Literacy is not a luxury, it is a right and a responsibility. If our world is to meet the challenges of the twenty-first century we must harness the energy and creativity of all our citizens."

- President Bill Clinton

"Parents should be encouraged to read to their children, and teachers should be equipped with all available techniques for teaching literacy, so the varying needs and capacities of individual kids can be taken into account."

- Hugh Mackay

CHAPTER I

IN THE MATTO GROSSO

The blood-red sun was sinking beyond the distant Geral Mountains, when a canoe, containing four white men and three natives, came to a halt a thousand miles from the mighty Amazon, in the upper waters of the Xingu River, near the great table-land of Matto Grosso.

It was hard work, forcing the long shallow boat against the rapid current of the stream, whose unknown source is somewhere among the famous diamond regions of Brazil. It was plain sailing for three hundred leagues from the Amazon, from whose majestic volume the little party of explorers had turned southward more than a month before. The broad sail, which was erected in the centre of the craft, swept it smoothly along over the narrowing bosom of the Xingu, between luxuriant forests and past tribes of strange-looking Indians, who stood on the banks staring wonderingly at the extraordinary beings, the like of which many of them had never seen before.

Occasionally the explorers put ashore, and, using only the language of signs, exchanged some of the beads and gaudy trinkets for the curious articles of the savages. Endless varieties of fruit were so abundant that it was to be had for the simple trouble of plucking; while the timid natives stood in such awe of their visitors, that the thought of harming them never entered their minds.

But ominous changes were gradually noted by our friends, as they steadily ascended the mysterious stream. At first the natives fled at their approach, and failed to understand the signs of comity, or were so distrustful of the strangers that they refused to meet their advances. Fleeing into the woods or high hills, they peeped out from their coverts, uttering strange cries and indulging in grotesque gestures, the meaning of which could hardly be mistaken. Had there been any misapprehension on the part of the visitors, there was none after several scores launched their arrows at the boat, as it glided away from the shore and up stream. The aim was wild and no one was struck, but when Professor Ernest Grimcke, the sturdy, blue-eyed scientist of the party, picked up one of the missiles and carefully examined it, he made the disturbing announcement that it was tipped with one of the deadliest of known poisons.

The other members of this exploring party were Fred Ashman, a bright, intelligent American, four-and-twenty years of age; Jared Long, an attenuated, muscular New Englander in middle life, and Aaron Johnston, a grim, reserved but powerful sailor from New Bedford, who had spent most of his life on whaling voyages. Professor Grimcke and Ashman were joint partners in the exploring enterprise, Long and Johnston being their assistants.

In addition, there were three native servants, or helpers, known as Bippo, Pedros and Quincal. They had been engaged at Macapa, near the mouth of the Amazon. They were rather small of size, the first-named being the most intelligent, and in that warm, tropical climate wore no clothing except a strip of native cloth around the loins.

Ashman had striven to teach them the use of firearms, but they could never overcome the terror caused by the jet of fire and the thunderous explosion when the things were discharged. They, therefore, clung to their spears, which, having honest points, cannot be said to have been very formidable weapons in their hands, even though each native was able to throw them with remarkable deftness and accuracy.

The sail that had served the explorers so well, where the Xingu was broader and with a slower current, became useless, or at least proved unequal to the task of overcoming the force of the stream. Consequently they had recourse to the broad-bladed oars, with which they drove the canoe swiftly against the resisting river, cheered by the oft-repeated declaration of the Professor, whose spirits never flagged, that the harder it proved going up stream, the easier must it be in descending, and that the arrangement was much better than if the condition of affairs were reversed.

The most tiresome work came when they reached some place, where the falls or rapids compelled them to land, and, lifting the boat and its contents from the ground, carry it round the obstruction to the more favorable current above. These portages varied in length from a few rods to a fourth of a mile, and the further the party advanced, the more frequent did they become.

"We have gone far enough for to-night," said the Professor, as the prow of the boat was turned toward the left bank; "we will go into camp and make ready for to-morrow."

A few minutes later, the bow of the canoe gently touched the dark sand of the shore. Bippo, Pedros and Quincal understood their duty so well that, without suggestion from the others, they leaped into the shallow waters, ran a few steps, and, grasping the front of the craft, drew it so far upon the land that the others stepped out without so much as wetting the soles of their shoes.

This task was no more than finished, when the natives scattered in the forest, which came almost to the edge of the water, in quest of fuel. This of course was so abundant that the work was slight, but since Professor Grimcke and Fred Ashman paid them well for their services they were left to attend to that duty unassisted.

As the surroundings of the party were entirely new and strange, Grimcke proposed that while the evening meal was being prepared, they should find out, if it could be done, whether any unwelcome neighbors were likely to disturb them before morning. After a brief consultation, it was decided that the Professor and Jared Long should make their way up the river, keeping close to shore, with the purpose of learning the extent of the rapids, while Ashman and the sailor, Johnston, should follow the clearly marked trail which led directly away from the stream and into the forest. It was more than probable that one of the couples would come upon something worth knowing, and it was not unlikely that both would return with important information.

Twilight is of short duration in the low latitudes, and the wish of the four white men was to be back in camp at the end of an hour, by which time night would be fairly upon them. But the moon was at its full and would serve them better than the twilight itself.

The German and New Englander, therefore, moved away from camp, following the course of the Xingu, while their two friends quickly vanished in the forest. Each carried his repeating Winchester and his Smith & Wesson.

Edward S. Ellis

Ashman felt some misgiving because of the trail leading into the woods from a point so near the camp. It seemed likely to have been worn by the inhabitants of some village near at hand, though it was possible that the innumerable feet of wild animals on their way to and from the river may have been the cause. The upper waters of the Xingu are remarkably clear and pure, a fact which rendered the first theory most probable.

The explorers had landed in a dangerous region, as they were destined to learn very soon, and the experience of the couples who took routes at right angles to each other was of the most thrilling character.

It has been stated that the progress of the canoe had been checked, as was often the case before, by the rapids of the Xingu, which could be passed only by carrying the canoe and luggage to the smoother waters above. It was apparent that the river frequently overflowed its banks, for immense quantities of driftwood lined both shores, while the vegetation had been swept away to that extent that a space of a dozen feet from the margin of the stream was comparatively free from it. Thus both parties found the travelling easy.

The rapids were a hundred yards wide, more or less, and, with such a steep incline, that the foamy waves dashed hither and thither and against each other with the utmost fury, sending the spray high in air and sweeping forward with such impetuosity that it seemed impossible for the strongest craft under the most skilful guidance to shoot them. The explorers studied them with great interest as they ascended the left bank.

It was inevitable that in a country with such excessive vegetable growth, every part of the Xingu should show much floating timber. The logs which plunged through the rapids played all manner of antics. Sometimes they leaped high out of the waters, like immense sea monsters, the out-spreading limbs showing a startling resemblance to the arms of a drowning person mutely appealing for help. Then a heavy trunk would strike a rock just below the surface, and the branches, dripping with spray, swept over in a huge semi-circle. The roar and swirl suggested the whirlpool below the falls of Niagara, one of the most appalling sights in all nature.

Edward S. Ellis

CHAPTER II

A TRIO OF ENEMIES

At last, when the full moon was shining, the two men stood at the head of the rapids and surveyed their surroundings before setting out on their return to camp.

Both sides of the Xingu were lined by the dense forest, in which the vegetation is so luxuriant that it must be a source of never ending wonder to those who look upon it for the first time. The river above made a sharp bend, shutting off the view so fully that from their position, it was impossible to tell how far they would be able to use the canoe without making another portage.

"We haven't seen a person on our way here," remarked the Professor, calmly surveying the river and shores; "and I hope Ashman will bring back a similar report, for we all need a full night's rest."

"How is *that*?"

Long touched the arm of his companion, as he asked the question, and pointed down stream in the direction of camp.

To the amazement of the Professor, three natives were seen

standing on the very spot where they themselves had stood a brief while before, evidently scrutinizing the white strangers with profound wonder and curiosity.

They were dressed similarly to Bippo, Pedros and Quincal—that is, with only a piece of cloth around the loins—but they displayed a marked contrast in other respects. They were taller, more athletic, with immense bushy heads of hair, enormous rings in their ears, while the hue of their skins was almost as dark as that of the native African.

One carried a long-bow and a bundle of arrows strapped behind his shoulders, while the others were armed simply with javelins or spears.

"Those fellows mean fight," added Long.

"No doubt of it," replied the Professor.

"But a Winchester will reach further than their arrows and spears, even if they are tipped with poison."

"Possibly they may be friendly, if they can be convinced that we intend them no harm, and you know what an advantage it will be to us if able to trust all the natives on our return."

Long could not share the confidence of his companion and favored a direct advance down the bank toward the savages. If the latter preserved their armed neutrality, all would be well enough, but at the first sign of hostility he advocated opening fire on them.

Perhaps he was right in the declaration that anything like timidity in dealing with savages is the worst possible course. While the rights of every barbarian should be respected, it is all important that he should know that such concession is

Edward S. Ellis

made not through fear, but because the superior party wishes to be just and merciful.

The natives stood as motionless as statues for several minutes, during which the white men scrutinized them with an interest that may be imagined.

The first and most natural thought of our friends was that an encounter could be avoided by entering the forest on the right and passing round the savages, who, it was quite apparent, intended to dispute their return; but if such was really their purpose, they would have little trouble in heading off the whites in the dense wood, beside which, for the weighty reasons already named, it would have been exceedingly unwise to act as though afraid of the dusky natives.

Despite Long's protest, the Professor decided to make a friendly advance, being vigilantly on his guard at the same time for the first offensive move of the savages. He carried his Winchester in one hand, while he rested the other on his revolver. He was determined, while hoping for comity, to be prepared for hostility or treachery.

Long was so dissatisfied with the looks of things, that he followed his friend a few paces, then halting with his Winchester ready for any emergency, and certain in his own mind that a sharp fight was inevitable.

The approach of the white man was evidently a surprise to the savages. The middle one, who held the long-bow and arrows, fell back several paces, as if about to break into flight or dart among the trees so invitingly near, but something must have been said by his companions to check him, for he stopped abruptly, and not only came back to his first position, but advanced a couple of paces beyond. The noise from the rapids prevented the Professor hearing their voices, though the unusually clear moonlight told him that some utterance had passed between them.

The first ominous act on the part of the natives was by this archer, who deliberately drew an arrow from over his shoulder and fitted it against the string of his bow. The fact that the missile was undoubtedly coated at the end with a virus more deadly than that of the rattlesnake or cobra was enough to render the would-be friend uncomfortable and to increase his alertness.

At the same time that the archer went through this significant preliminary, his companions shifted their grasp upon their javelins in a manner that was equally suggestive.

While carrying these primitive weapons, the fingers closed around the centre of gravity, that naturally being more convenient, but when about to hurl them, the hand was shoved further toward the head. Both natives thus shifted their right hands, though, they still held them horizontal at their thighs, from which position they could be brought aloft in the twinkling of an eye.

The white man walked slowly. The left hand, which supported his rifle, remained motionless, but removing the right from his revolver, he continued making signs, whose friendly meaning was so obvious that it was impossible for the natives to mistake it.

While approaching in this guarded manner, he Studied them with the closest scrutiny. Interesting under any circumstances, they were vastly more so at this time. What struck him in addition to the characteristics already named, were their frowsy eyebrows and glittering coal-black eyes. These were unusually large and protruding. The noses, instead of

Edward S. Ellis

being broad and flat, like those of the native Africans, were Roman in shape. The mouths were wide, and, when they spoke, he observed that the teeth which were displayed were black, showing that a fashion prevailed among this unknown tribe similar to that in vogue among many of the natives in the East Indies.

Now, Professor Grimcke was too experienced an explorer to walk directly into danger, where there was no prospect of avoiding a desperate encounter. While eager to make friends with all the people whom he met, he did not intend to assume any unnecessary risks. The demeanor of the natives tendered it certain they were hostile. They made no responsive signs to those of the white man, and the latter would have checked himself half way, but for his suspicion that they were mystified by his conduct and were undecided as to the precise thing to do.

He not only heard their peculiar rumbling voices, but saw from the movements of their lips and their glances in each other's faces, that they were consulting as to what they should do. The white man was already so close that he could easily be reached by the bowman, and there was little doubt that either of the others could hurl his poisoned javelin the intervening distance.

The only way of defeating such a movement was for the white man to secure "the drop" on them, but, in one sense that was impossible. Unable to understand the words spoken, they were equally unacquainted with the weapons of the pale face, and would, doubtless pay no heed to the most threatening demonstration on his part.

"Take my advice and come back," called Jared Long; "keep your face toward them and blaze away, and I'll do my part!"

Instead of adopting the suggestion of his friend, the Professor slowed his pace, still making his gestures of good will. However, when fifty steps away, he came to a dead halt.

He had advanced three-fourths the distance, and, if the others were willing to accept his offers, they should signify it by coming forward and meeting him where he had stopped.

While moving forward in this guarded manner, Grimcke was prudent enough to edge over toward the woods, which were now so close to his right side as to be instantly available. When he came to a stop also it was near the trunk of a large tree, no more than a yard distant.

"The Professor is cunning," reflected Jared Long, watching every movement; "he'll whisk behind the tree the instant one of them makes a move. Helloa! what's up now?"

To the astonishment of both white men the native with the bow shifted it at this moment to his right hand, holding the arrow in place against the string with the same hand, while the weapon was at his side. Then he moved a step or two, as if to meet the stranger.

"Look out!" called the vigilant New Englander, "that chap is up to some deviltry."

He did not refer to him with the bow and arrow, but to one of the others, who stealthily turned aside and vanished among the trees. Being in the Professor's line of vision the latter observed the suspicious movement, and it cannot be said that it added to his comfort.

Meanwhile the archer advanced, but with such tardy step that it was evident he was timing his pace to that of his comrade who had so stealthily entered the wood. Convinced that his real peril lay among those trees, Grimcke began a backward movement with such caution that he hoped it would not be noticed by the native who was approaching with a sluggish pace.

The forest, like all those in South America, was so dense that great care was necessary for one to pick his way through it. The Professor's theory was that the savage with the spear would regulate his movements on the theory that the white man would not stir from the place where he had first halted. He would thus aim to secure a position from which he could hurl his javelin at him without detection. Grimcke conceived this was certain to take place, and, if he remained where he was, nothing could save him from the treacherous assault. It was a matter, therefore, of self preservation that dictated the brief retreat with the hope of thus disconcerting the savage.

The task which Grimcke had given himself was difficult indeed. The ground was unfavorable for the peculiar twitching movement which he hoped would carry him out of danger. He had gone barely a couple of yards when the bowman evidently suspected something of the kind, for he stopped short and stared inquiringly at the white man.

The latter extended his right hand as if to shake that of the savage, who stood motionless, making no sign of pleasure or displeasure. Indeed, he remained so fixed in his position that Grimcke was convinced he was listening for the sound of the other miscreant stealing through the wood. He plainly saw the black eyes cast a single inquiring glance in that direction.

"This is getting a little too threatening," reflected the Professor, satisfied that the three natives were as venomous as so many serpents; "at the first move war is declared."

His situation was so critical that he did not dare turn his head to look behind him, but never was there a more welcome sound to him than that made by the footsteps of the lank New Englander.

"Keep moving hack!" called Long, "but don't try to hide what you're doing."

The Professor saw the sense of this advice and he followed it, lifting his feet so high that the action was plainly seen, but doing so with a certain dignity that was not lacking in impressiveness. His aim was to give the act the appearance of a strategic movement, as it may be called. It was not that he was afraid of the natives, but he was seeking a better place from which to open hostilities against them.

This was the impression which he sought to give the fierce savages, and whether he succeeded, or not was certain to become apparent within the following five minutes. He himself believed, the chances were against the success of his plan.

CHAPTER III

LIVELY WORK

Now took place an unprecedented incident.

The air of comity, or at least neutrality, which brooded over the two parties had given way to that of silent but intense hostility. The prowling movement of the native with the spear as he slipped into the wood, the sudden advance of Jared Long, whose face became like a thunder-cloud, when every hope of a friendly termination vanished, and the abrupt halt of the bowman, showed that all parties had thrown off the cloak of good will and become deadly enemies.

The third savage kept his place farther down the stream, his black eyes fixed on the archer in front, while he doubtless was waiting for some action on the part of his comrade who had stolen into the wood. As has been stated, he was nigh enough to hurl his javelin, so that both the white men were too wise to eliminate him from the curiously involved problem that confronted them.

The bowman having halted, stood a moment with his piercing black eyes fixed on the nearest white man, as if seeking to read in his face the meaning of his action or rather abrupt cessation of action.

"Professor," called Jared, "I'll attend to the one in front of you; but look out for the scamp among the trees."

Grimcke was relieved to hear this, and had there been only the two natives to confront, he would have been disturbed by no misgiving, but there were signs that the third one down the stream was preparing to do his part in the treacherous business. He too began advancing, but instead of doing so with the quick, angry stride of the New Englander, he stepped slowly and softly, as if seeking to conceal his movement.

Grimcke would have been glad to turn the archer over to the care of Long, but he was so frightfully close, that he did not dare do so. A moment's delay on the part of his friend would be fatal. At the same time, it was not to be forgotten that the most stealthy foe of all was prowling among the trees on the right.

The Professor's hope, as has been explained, was that his own retrogression had disconcerted the plans of this special miscreant for whom, however, he kept a keen watch.

The archer still held his bow, with the arrow in place grasped by his right hand, the long weapon resting against his hip. Provided he was right-handed, the bow would have to be shifted to his left hand, the arrow drawn back with the right and the missile then launched at his foe. This, it would seem, involved enough action to give both Grimcke and Long abundance of time in which to anticipate him.

But there remained the possibility that the savage was left-handed, in which event, the necessary action on his part would be much less, though sufficiently complicated to afford the white men abundance of time to anticipate him.

Edward S. Ellis

The native *was* left-handed, with a quickness that surpassed all expectation, the bow was suddenly raised, the end of the arrow drawn back and the missile driven directly at the breast of Grimcke.

At precisely the same instant, the latter's strained ear caught the crackling of a twig, above the din of the rapids (which was much less there than below), and something was discerned moving among the trees on his right. His frightened glance in that direction gave him a glimpse of a dusky figure in the act of hurling his javelin.

Thus it was that the spearman and archer let fly at precisely the same instant, and Jared Long, who was so anxious to help his friend, saw only the deft movements of the archer. Grimcke could not fire at both in time to save himself, but he instinctively did the very best and indeed the only thing that could be done. Without moving his feet, he dropped to a sitting posture, instantly popping up again like a jack-in-the-box.

The movement took place at precisely the right instant, and both the javelin and arrow whizzed over his head, without grazing him, but the arrow shot by Long's temple so close that he blinked and for an instant believed he had been hit.

But, like the hunter when bitten by a rattlesnake, he determined to crush his assailant and to attend to his hurt afterwards.

The sharp crack of the Winchester, the shriek of the smitten savage and his frenzied leap in the air, followed in such instant succession that they seemed simultaneous. When the wretch went back on the ground he was as dead as Julius Caesar.

A man can fire with amazing rapidity, when using a Winchester repeater, but some persons are like cats in their own movements. The New Englander leveled his weapon as quickly as he could bring it to his shoulder, but the native along the side of the Xingu had vanished as though he never existed.

Whether he knew anything about fire-arms or not, he was quick to understand that some kind of weapon in the hands of the white men had knocked the bowman out of time, and he bounded among the trees at his side, as though he, too, was discharged from the bow. He was just quick enough to escape the bullet that would have been after him an instant later.

The moment Grimcke knew that he was safe from the javelin, which sped over his head, he straightened up, and, still maintaining his removable posture, discharged his gun at the point whence came the well-nigh fatal missile.

But the shot was a blind one, for he did not see the native at the instant of firing. Nothing could have surpassed the alertness of these strange savages. The one with the javelin disappeared with the same suddenness as did his brother down the bank, and, had the archer but comprehended his danger he, too, would have escaped.

The affray roused the wrath of both Long and Grimcke. They had offered the hand of friendship, only to be answered with an attempt upon their lives. One of their assailants had eluded them, and the other would have been an assailant had the opportunity been given.

"Let's shoot him too!"

He alluded to the man who hurled the javelin and who, so far as they could see, was left without any weapon with which to defend himself. In their natural excitement over their victory, the friends forgot themselves for the moment. Heedless of consequences, they dashed among the trees, in pursuit of the savage who had flung his spear with well-nigh fatal effect.

The undergrowth was frightfully tangled, and, as the first plunge, the Professor went forward on his hands and knees. The wonder was how Long kept his feet; but it will be remembered that he was much more attenuated than his companion, and seemed to have picked up a skill elsewhere which now stood him well.

The moon was shining and despite the dense vegetation around him, enough rays found their way to the ground to give him a partial view for few paces in front. He had not gone far when he caught a glimpse of the dusky figure slipping through the undergrowth ahead, and at no great distance.

Strange as it may seem, the impetuosity of the American caused him to gain upon the terrified native, who, having flung his poisoned weapon, was without the means of defending himself. It was not in the nature of things, however, that Long should overtake the fugitive, who was more accustomed to making his way through such obstructions. The first burst of pursuit caused the white man to believe he would win in the strange race, but the next minute he saw he was losing ground.

Determined that the wretch should not escape, he checked his pursuit for an instant, and, bringing his Winchester to his shoulder, let fly.

But brief as was his halt, it give the savage time to make one terrific bound which shut him almost from sight, and rendered the hasty aim of Long so faulty that his intended victim was not so much as scratched.

Had the savage dashed deeper into the forest, he would have passed beyond all peril at this moment, but he was seeking to do that which Long did not discover until after discharging his gun. He headed toward the river, where he was first seen. It must have been that he was actuated by a desire to go to the help of his comrade, or more likely he was anxious to recover his javelin, in which he placed unbounded faith, and believed he could do it without undue risk.

Whatever his purpose, he quickly burst from the forest, while Long, who was pushing furiously after him, discovered from the increasing light in front, that he was close to the Xingu again.

Suspecting his purpose, the white man tore forward at the most reckless speed, and, before the native could recover his weapon and dart back to cover, he himself had dashed into the moonlight.

"Now, we've got him!" he shouted; "there's no getting away *this* time!"

This exultant exclamation was uttered to a form which appeared on his right, and who he was certain was the Professor; but to his consternation, as he turned his head, he saw that it was the other native, javelin in hand!

Edward S. Ellis

CHAPTER IV

HOW IT ENDED

It will be recalled that the Professor started in pursuit of the flying native with as much ardor as his friend, but, less skilful than he, he had taken but a step or two, when an obstruction flung him to the ground with discouraging emphasis.

Concluding that he had undertaken a futile task, he hastily climbed to his feet to await the return of Long who, he was satisfied, would attempt only a brief pursuit.

Remembering the javelin which had whizzed so near his crown, he cast about for a moment and picked it up from the earth where it lay but a few feet distant. As he balanced it in his hand, he observed that it was about six feet in length, was made entirely of wood, which was heavy and as hard and smooth as polished ebony.

The light of the moon was like that of the day itself. It would have been easy to read ordinary print by it. He had no trouble, therefore, in closely examining the novel implement of war. As he suspected, the point was made of stone or flint, ground almost to needle-like sharpness and securely fastened in place by a fine tendon wound around the portion of the stick that held the harder part. This was covered with a gummy substance extending to the end.

This he was satisfied was among the most virulent of substances known to toxicology. A puncture of the skin was sure to be fatal unless some remedy, of whose existence he held no suspicion, was instantly obtainable.

He had set down his rifle white examining the weapon, but quickly caught it up again, still retaining the javelin in his right band. He had been startled by the sound of the terrific threshing among the trees on his right.

He supposed that his friend was coming back, but, glancing toward the point where he expected him to appear, he was amazed to see the third native, who whisked off before Long could draw a bead on him, step from the wood not twenty paces away. His back was toward the Professor, and, strangely enough, he did not observe the white man—an oversight that never could have occurred, but for the tumult in the undergrowth which held his attention.

Grimcke had hardly caught sight of him, when the other native came flying to view, so astonishing his waiting comrade that he stood a moment irresolute after the white pursuer burst into sight.

Brief as was this pause, it gave the Professor time for some exceedingly fine work. He uttered a shout which caused the native to turn his affrighted gaze behind him, just in time to observe the white man with javelin raised and apparently in the very act of launching it at him.

The savage knew what a prick from that frightful thing meant, and with a howling shriek he ducked his head as though he had caught its whizz through the air, and shot among the trees with as much celerity as his companion had shown in coming from them.

Neither of the explorers wished to slay the natives, no matter how savage, unless compelled to do so in actual self-defence. Long had recovered from his first burst of fury, and, though the Professor could have sunk the javelin in the naked body, he withheld it, not unwilling that his assailant, now that he had started to flee, should escape.

The one who had so foolishly come back to the river side was left in the worst possible situation, for both his enemies stood between him and the sheltering forest and he was defenceless. He was at their mercy, and such people as those natives neither gave nor expected quarter, when engaged in their savage warfare.

The fellow acted like a bewildered animal. The white strangers were standing a few paces apart, so as to form the two angles of a triangle, while he made the third. The nearest point to the forest way midway between Grimcke and Long, as was apparent to the savage, who was fairly cornered.

Had the Xingu behind him been as placid as farther above or below the rapids, he would not have hesitated to plunge into its waters, trusting to his skill in swimming; but, to dive into the raging current would have been as certain destruction as for a man to undertake to swim unaided through the whirlpool below Niagara.

Grimcke and Long were not unwilling to torment the fellow, because of his cowardly attempt a few minutes before, though, as has been stated, neither intended to do him any special harm.

The affrighted native crouched down, as though seeking to

draw himself into such a narrow compass that the terrible javelin could not reach him. Despite the proof he had seen of the power of the civilized weapons, he held his own in greater dread.

Grimcke raised the spear, as if poising it aloft to hurl at the savage. The latter uttered a howl of terror, and, with his head still low, attempted to dart between the strangers. Naturally he shied as far away as possible from the Professor, and thereby brought himself almost close enough to touch Jared.

"That's what I want," muttered the latter, hurriedly concentrating his strength in his good right leg, and delivering the most powerful kick at his command.

It was well aimed and most effectively landed. The Professor was sure he heard the "dull thud," and always insisted that the recipient was lifted clear of the ground and propelled among the trees with an impetus sufficient to break his neck.

"There!" exclaimed the New Englander, looking around, "I guess I'm through!"

"I am sure that last fellow hopes so," said the Professor with a laugh, "for it's safe to conclude he was never handled with such vigor before."

The levity which both felt over their triumphant routing of their assailants was checked by the sight of the stark, lifeless form on the ground, only a few paces distant.

They had the best plea in the world for shooting the fierce savage, but the consciousness that the necessity existed and that the deed had been done, rendered them serious and thoughtful.

Edward S. Ellis

There was reason for believing the other natives would watch them from the forest, and the one who retained his javelin was likely to seek the chance to use it again. He certainly had strong temptation to do so, with the prospect of little risk to himself.

Besides, as the explorers followed the rapids, their uproar increased to that extent that the savages could move freely without danger of any noise being overheard.

The most prudent thing to do seemed for the friends to walk so briskly as to disconcert any plan their enemies might have formed. This was quite easy, because of the open space, already mentioned, as lining both banks of the Xingu.

Fortunately the distance to camp was not far, and, with the hurried pace adopted by the Professor and Long, it ought not to occupy more than a few minutes, provided no interruption occurred. Strange emotions tortured both, as they kept their eyes fixed on the dark wood at their side, from which they expected the sweep of the fearful javelin, whose touch was death.

The keenest hearing could not detect the faint whizz, while the roar of the rapids was in their ears, and they had to depend, therefore, on their eyes, which promised to be of little more service.

But the entire distance was almost passed, and the hearts of the two were beating high with increasing hope, when Long, with a gasp of terror, grasped the arm of the Professor with incredible force, and jerking him backward, pointed with his extended finger to the camp in front of them.

CHAPTER V

THE NATIVE VILLAGE

Meanwhile, Fred Ashman and Aaron Johnston the sailor, found themselves involved in a most stirring experience.

After studying the path or trail which led directly from the camp into the vast forest, stretching to an unknown distance from the Xingu, the young man decided to follow the route which he believed had been formed by persons instead of the wild animals of the wilderness.

Johnston was disposed to complain, but he was deeply attached to the manly partner in the exploring enterprise, and there was no reasonable peril which he would not willingly face in his defence.

The forest wore an unusually gloomy and dismal appearance, now that the sun had set and night was closing in.

The roar of the rapids, which at first sounded so loud, grew duller and fainter as they penetrated the wood until it became like the moaning of the distant ocean. The men spoke in guarded undertones and were able to hear each other plainly, while eyes and ears were on the alert, for the first sight or sound of danger.

Edward S. Ellis

Being within the forest, they were favored with but little of the moonlight, which proved such a help to their friends in their ascent of the bank of the Xingu to the head of the rapids. But here and there a few of the rays penetrated the vegetation overhead and illuminated the trail sufficiently to prevent their wandering from it.

Ashman was less than a rod in advance of the sailor and led until they had traversed perhaps a fifth of a mile, during which they met no living creature, though the noises from the wood left no doubt that wild animals were on every hand.

Fred began to think he had gone far enough, though his wish to obtain a glimpse of the village, which he believed was not far off, prevented his coming to a full stop. Johnston noticing his hesitation put in another vigorous protest, but he was easily persuaded to venture further under the pledge that if they discovered nothing within the next ten minutes, they would withdraw and return to camp.

Knowing that his companion would insist on the fulfillment of this agreement, Fred pushed on faster than before; the sailor, however, easily maintaining his place almost on his heels. It was only at intervals they spoke, for there was no call to do so, and it was not wise to allow any cause to interfere with their watchfulness for the peril which was liable to come with the suddenness of the thunderbolt.

By stepping carefully they were able to proceed without noise, and, at the same time, hoped to catch the sound of any other footsteps, since there was not supposed to be any call on the part of the natives for the caution which they might have displayed under different circumstances.

The young man's heart gave a quicker throb than usual when he caught the sound of something like a shout, and observed a faint light in the path in front. It was apparent that the latter made an abrupt turn, and the cause of the noise was but a brief distance beyond.

Fred reached back his hand and touched his companion, as a warning for the most extreme care on his part, but the admonition was not needed. Johnston understood the situation too well.

Sure enough, less than a couple of rods further, and the path turned almost at right angles. Passing guardedly around this, the explorers came upon a striking scene.

There was an open space with an area of perhaps three or four acres; it was as clear of trees as a stretch of western prairie. It was triangular in shape, the boundary being so regular that there could be no doubt it was artificially made.

Around three sides of this space were erected huts or cabins, the excellence and similarity or their structure suggesting that the natives were the superior in intelligence of any that had yet been encountered during the ascent of the Xingu. The huts were a dozen feet square, half as high, and each had a broad open entrance in the middle of the front. They seemed to be built of logs or heavy limbs, the roofs being flat and composed of the branches of trees, overlaid with leaves and earth.

In the middle of the open square was a tall pole, like an immense flag-staff. The light which had been noticed sometime before by the whites was the full flood of the moon's rays, there being no other kind of illumination, so far as they could ascertain, in the native village.

The huge pole was without any limbs or appurtenances, but around the space were gathered a score of figures in rapid motion, the meaning of whose actions was a puzzle to the white spectators, until they studied them.

Then it was seen they were struggling together, and the conclusion was that they were engaged in some kind of a rough sport, for all the rest of the savages were seated in front of their huts watching the singular spectacle.

Naturally they ought to have come closer, and the fact that they did not, suggested that they kept back to give the actors plenty of room for their performances.

Not the least impressive feature of the scene was the profound silence which marked it. The shout that first arrested the attention of Ashman and his companion, must have been some kind of a signal, probably announcing the opening of the proceedings.

It was evident that the villagers in the square were struggling hard, for their forms were interlocked and they were divided into two lines, which swayed back and forth as one gained or yielded ground.

"It is a wrestling bout," whispered Ashman to his companion, and then, reflecting that their situation was dangerous, the two stopped from the path among the trees, where they would not be noticed by any passing near.

Suddenly something like a groan was heard from the body of contesting men. Almost at the same instant, a command was shouted from the further end of the square, where part of the spectators were gathered. The two lines fell apart, and ran silently and swiftly to opposite points a hundred feet distant, where they abruptly halted as if in obedience to some signal and faced each other.

This was stirring enough, but that which riveted the eyes of the white men was the sight of three figures lying prone on the ground, at the foot of the pole.

They were as motionless as so many stones. There could be no mistaking the significance of the sight: they were dead.

It may have been some species of sport in which the actors were engaged for the entertainment of the spectators, but, if so, there was an awful earnestness about it, for the stake for which they strove was human life.

The two lines faced each other but a moment, when another shout rang out, and they rushed together once more with the fury of two cyclones.

By this time, our friends had discovered that no member of the parties was furnished with any weapon other than those provided by nature.

Fearful then must have been the struggle, which had already terminated in the death of three of the contestants.

But they were at it again with the fierceness of so many cougars fighting in defence of their young.

The result was terrifying. The contest had lasted but a few minutes, and already a couple were on the earth, when one of the combatants, with a cry of pain dashed in almost a direct line toward the spot where our friends were hiding.

Had he not been overtaken and dragged back, he would have been upon them before they could get out of the way, and it is not difficult to conjecture what would have followed.

The miserable wretch, however, was seized on the very edge

of the wood by four others and carried writhing and resisting back to the space. There he was flung down, and, being unable to rise, the others leaped upon him and in a few minutes all was over. He was added to the list that were already *hors du combat*.

Ashman and Johnston had received a shock which drove away all interest in the fearful spectacle. Their escape was exceedingly narrow and they could scarcely hope for such good fortune again.

Fred touched his friend and whispered to him. Immediately, they began stealing from the dangerous spot.

CHAPTER VI

ALONG THE FOREST PATH

If any further proof were needed of the delicacy and danger of the situation of the white men, it came the next minute, when, as they were in the act of stepping back into the trail, the sailor caught the arm of his friend and checked him.

No need of speaking, for Ashman had detected the peril at the same instant.

Two natives were stealing like phantoms along the path, from the direction of the river and going toward the village.

Had they been ten seconds later, the foremost would have collided with the young explorer.

The latter held his breath, and placed his hand on his revolver, believing a fight was inevitable.

So it would have been, had not the attention of the savages been absorbed by the scene in the square, of which they caught sight a pace or two before coming opposite the watchers.

They strode directly onward, and swung across the open

Edward S. Ellis

space, swerving enough to one side to avoid the struggling lines, and moving on until they reached the fringe of spectators beyond. There they could no longer be identified, and probably took their places among those who were enjoying the cruel spectacle.

Ashman waited a brief while beside the path, fearful that other natives might be coming; but, when the minutes passed without their appearance, he resumed picking his way back, and quickly stood erect in the narrow opening, which he felt had been followed too far from the Xingu.

There was no reason to suspect that any of the natives knew of the presence of the mysterious strangers so near them, but since they seemed to have a remarkable disposition to be on the move, our friends felt it would not be safe to relax their caution for a single instant.

While they did not apprehend a direct pursuit, there was a probability that some parties might be moving along the trail behind them, while they had seen enough to convince them of the danger from the front. Ashman, therefore, whispered to his companion to keep special guard against an approach from the rear, while he would be equally alert in guarding the front.

The two kept so near that they could have reached each other by simply extending the hand.

They had no more than fairly started on their withdrawal from the spot, when Johnston touched the arm of his friend, who instantly halted to learn the cause.

"I believe some of 'em are following us," said Johnston.

Fred listened, but his straining ear could detect nothing to warrant such an alarming conclusion, and he so stated.

The sailor became convinced that possibly he was mistaken. There is no law governing noises at night, and it might be that he had misjudged the rustling of a branch or possibly the stealthy footsteps of some wild animal.

Not entirely convinced, however, that his companion was mistaken, Fred once more resumed the advance, trying to perform the difficult task of giving as much attention to the rear as the front.

If the savages suspected the presence of others, they would be likely to tread so lightly that their footfalls could not be heard; but inasmuch as neither of the whites could believe they had even the most shadowy knowledge of them, they relied more on hearing than sight.

Suddenly Fred started and almost uttered an exclamation. In his nervous, apprehensive state, he was sure that one of their dusky foes had leaped from the side of the path and was crouching in front.

He drew his pistol and waited for the assault, which he was confident would come the next moment; but the seconds passed and all remained profoundly still.

With his weapon ready for instant use, he advanced a pace or two, touching the sailor as a command for him to remain motionless; but the chivalrous fellow would not obey, and was close behind him, when he stooped down and placed his hand on a piece of decayed limb that had fallen into the path.

"What a mistake," muttered Fred, with a sigh, as he shoved it aside with his foot, explaining its nature to the wondering Johnston.

But it was only simple prudence to maintain unceasing vigilance, and he did not permit the error to lessen his watchfulness. It was rather the reverse.

But the explorers were threading their way through a labyrinth of peril, the like of which they had never encountered before.

Fred had not gone a hundred yards further, when his companion once more caught his arm, and he turned about as before to learn the cause.

"What have you heard?" he asked, with his mouth almost against the ear of the other.

"There are some of 'em behind us, certain sure!"

"How do you know there are more than one?"

"By the sound—there!"

The amazement of the two may be understood, when they not only detected the sound of footfalls, but discovered that instead of being at the rear as both thought, they were in front!

A party of natives were approaching from the Xingu, and the keener hearing of Johnston first discovered them.

The whites had stopped near a spot where a few rays of moonlight fell upon the trail, giving them a faint but needed view of the direction from which the danger threatened.

Neither spoke again, but with the utmost care and noiselessness, they stepped aside from the path and crouched among the undergrowth.

They had barely time to ensconce themselves in their new position, when the footfalls sounded more distinctly than before, and something in the nature of an exclamation was heard from one of the approaching savages.

It sounded more like the grunt of a pig than anything the listeners could call to mind, and Ashman feared it was notice of one warrior to his companions that he had discovered something amiss.

But if such were the fact, the natives would have stopped, while the cat-like steps were more audible than before, though the wonder to the watchers was that the parties continued invisible.

The eyes of both remained fixed on the faintly illuminated space, where they expected to catch sight of them, but the straining gaze failed to detect the most shadowy form.

Ashman was just beginning to suspect some strange mistake had been made, when he suddenly saw the form of a tall savage with bushy head and a javelin in his hand, glide like a shadow into the darkness in front. A moment after, a second followed, then a third, fourth and fifth, the last carrying a long-bow, and all plainly seen by the whites at the side of the trail.

A few minutes later, Fred once more took the advance, reflecting that they were as likely to meet more of the natives as to have them overtake them.

The mystery was where they had come from in the first place. They could not have entered the trail at the camp where Ashman and Johnston had started on their little exploring enterprise. It looked as though they were hiding among the trees at the time the canoe approached the land,

Edward S. Ellis

and may have followed the explorers soon after they started along the path with the purpose of cutting off their retreat. If such should prove to be the case, Fred felt that not only he and his companion were in danger, but all the rest were liable to be attacked by these natives, who, as has been stated, were the most athletic that had been encountered since leaving the Amazon.

"Fred," whispered the sailor a little later, "they've turned back and are following us again."

"Are you sure of it?"

"There's no mistake about it."

Fred was debating whether they should not turn again from the path, but he reflected that the natives having discovered the trick played on them, would be likely to defeat such a piece of strategy.

Before he could decide upon the best course, Johnston whispered:

"Run! it's the only chance we've got!"

CHAPTER VII

DESPERATE WORK

It seemed to be the only course left. Whether it was or not, it was too late to try anything else. That the natives had discovered the explorers was proven by several low, tremulous whistles which at that instant sounded on the night.

It was risky running along the dark trail, even though illuminated here and there by the rays of the moon: but, feeling that the situation was desperate, Ashman broke into a swift lope, with Johnston at his heels, urging him to make haste.

"If they come too close," thought the young man, "we can dodge among the trees again and pick our way back to the river as best we can—helloa! what's that?"

Well might he ask himself the question, for the whizz of something close to his ear left no doubt that one of their pursuers had hurled a poisoned javelin at them.

An instant after he heard a faint but peculiar noise which he could not describe nor identify. Johnston at the same instant uttered a suppressed exclamation, not intended for his ears,

Edward S. Ellis

and he called out in a recklessly loud voice,

"Into the woods, quick!"

Ashman did not hesitate, but darted to his right, halting after a couple of steps, through fear of betraying himself.

"Where are you?" asked Johnston, speaking more guardedly.

His groping hand touched Ashman, who seized it and silently drew him forward, neither speaking again.

Even in that trying moment, the younger was impressed by the singularity of his friend's actions, though there was no opportunity to ask an explanation.

The savages could be plainly heard, as they hurried past, evidently believing they would overtake the fugitives the next minute and certain of locating them, wherever they might be.

Sure enough, they had not gone fifty feet, when they detected the trick and turned about to catch the whites before they could steal any distance from the trail.

"We must leave," said Ashman; "we are too close to the path, and they are sure to find us."

Johnston made no answer, and, instead of following him, sank heavily to the ground, with a groan.

"Great heaven! what is the matter, Aaron?" gasped his friend.

"I'm done for," was the feeble reply; "never mind me: look— out—for—for—good-bye!"

Struck almost dumb by an awful fear, Fred forgot the natives for the time and stooped over his friend. It was as he suspected; the poor fellow had been struck full in the back by one of the poisoned javelins. The exclamation which he uttered at the moment of receiving the wound was that which puzzled Ashman. The sailor had withdrawn the weapon, and the wound bled but little. The young man, however, identified it on the instant.

"Aaron, rouse up!" he called, shaking his shoulder; "fight off your drowsiness!"

He suddenly ceased, for at that moment, he realized that his companion was dead. Thus fearfully did the virus do its work.

Before Ashman, could do more than rally from his shock, a muttered exclamation at his elbow announced that the savages had located him.

"Curse you!" he exclaimed, whipping out his revolver and letting fly in the dark at the point where he knew several of his foes were standing, waiting for a chance to hurl their missiles at him.

A screech announced that the bullet had found its mark, and he followed it with a couple more shots, which inflicted wounds, even if they caused no mortal ones.

The effect of this volley was to throw the natives into consternation and panic. There is nothing go appalling as an unknown peril, and the flashes of fire lighting up the gloom sent them flying toward their village.

The path was open for the young man's escape, but could he leave the body of his friend behind?

Alas! it was that all he could do, and unless that were done within the next few minutes, it would be too late.

Stooping over, he grasped the shoulders of the body and drew it further from the path, in the hope that it would remain unnoticed. Then he loosed the Winchester from the death grip, removed the revolver, and stepping back into the trail, started on his sorrowful return to his friends.

"I wish they would follow me," he muttered; glaring into the gloom behind him; "the man they have killed is worth more than the whole tribe of miscreants."

He was in a savage mood, and, despite the fearful danger from the poisoned arrows and spears, he yearned for another chance at the wretches who fought so unfairly.

He held a couple of loaded and repeating Winchesters, with which he could pour the most destructive of volleys among the savages, and he longed for the opportunity; but the profound silence which followed the fierce encounter was so striking that to Fred it all seemed like some horrid vision of sleep.

But he dare not wait. These wretches had come from the direction of the Xingu, and he was apprehensive of trouble at the camp, where the three native attendants had been left. His services might be needed at that very moment.

He did not run, but advanced with the stealth of an American Indian stealing upon an enemy. It seemed to him his senses were strung to a higher pitch than ever before, for he had not walked far, when he became aware that some one was ahead of him, in the path and travelling in the same direction.

As yet he could catch no glimpse of the stranger, but there

could be no mistake about the stealthy tread. He was sure, too, that sooner or later the broken rays of moonlight would give him the sight for which he was waiting.

"Yonder is a spot where he will betray himself," he added a moment later, as he observed the faint light ahead.

Instead of following on, Fred paused and laying the rifle of his dead friend on the ground he knelt and sighted his own piece as best he could in the darkness. Where the hunter is placed in such a situation he instinctively *feels* how to aim his weapon.

He was not kept long waiting. A dark form became dimly outlined in the faint moonlight and an instant later the infuriated Ashman fired.

The rasping screech which followed was enough to curdle one's blood, but the young man only uttered an exclamation of disgust. He had driven a ball through the vitals of a South American cougar, instead of through one of the natives, a score of whom he gladly would have wiped out of existence had he possessed the power.

The shot could not have been better aimed, had the sun been shining. The furious beast dropped in the middle of the path, rolled over on his back, clawed the air for a moment or two, and then became motionless. Had not Ashman been on the lookout when he reached the spot, he would have stumbled over the carcass.

"It is only so much ammunition thrown away," he muttered, again glaring into the gloom behind him, in the hope of catching sight or sound of his pursuers; but they were too thoroughly panic-stricken by the frightful experience a few minutes before to trouble the white man for some time

　　　　Edward S. Ellis

to come.

The dull roar of the rapids grew plainer, and, increasing his pace, he had but to walk a short distance when the clear moonlight, unobstructed by cloud or vegetation, was discerned where the path debouched from the forest.

The feeling that something had gone amiss in the camp during his absence was so strong with Ashman that he slowed his walk and stopped before emerging from the wood. He paused, however, at a point where he had a full view not only of the camp but of the river and dark shore beyond.

The sight which met his gaze was not calculated to soothe his nerves. From some cause Bippo, Pedros and Quincal seemed to have been seized with a panic, hardly less than that produced among their countrymen by the discharge of the firearms of Ashman. They were in the act of shoving the canoe back into the water in such haste that there could be no doubt they intended to flee from some enemy that had driven all thoughts of resistance out of their minds.

"What the mischief are you doing?" shouted the young man, dashing from cover and hurrying down the bank to intercept them before they could get away.

CHAPTER VIII

THE LAND OF MYSTERY

The peremptory tones of Fred Ashman rang out loud and clear above the roar of the rapids and caused the servants to halt at the moment the canoe was shoved into the water. They looked up with frightened expressions and awaited his approach.

"What do you mean?" he demanded as he drew near.

Bippo, who was by far the brightest of the three, had shown a wonderful readiness in picking up a knowledge of the English tongue. He was so much superior in that respect to his companions, that they invariably left to him the duty of conversing with their masters.

"*Dey're* ober dere," he replied, pointing to the other shore.

"Who's over there?"

"Perfess'r and Long man; we seed 'em, dey motion for us to hurry ober to 'em."

This was astounding news and Ashman was mystified.

Edward S. Ellis

"How did they get over there? And why did they leave camp?"

"Don' know; seed 'em; want us hurry."

Without waiting to reflect upon the strange information, and recalling that more of the natives were likely to issue from the path at any moment, the young man stepped into the canoe, and, catching up one of the paddles, lent his help in propelling the craft across the foamy Xingu.

"Where Johns'n?" asked Bippo, when the middle of the stream was reached, and without ceasing his toil with the paddle.

"The natives killed him with a poisoned spear; you will never see him again."

Bippo made no reply, but communicated the startling tidings to his companions, who muttered their amazement. It was apparent that the news had added to their panic, and they bent to their task with such vigor that the boat rapidly approached the other bank.

Fred was asking himself, that if his friends had managed to get across the river, why it was they were not in sight. He scrutinized the dark forest and the line of moonlit space in the expectation, of seeing them come forth to welcome him, but not a soul was in sight.

He did not know what to make of it. There was something so uncanny about the whole business, that a strange distrust and uneasiness took possession of him. It could not be that the natives had deceived him and were anxious to place the Xingu between them and the fierce savages who had handled the whites so roughly. Bippo and his comrades had shown a loyalty from the first which gave their employers the fullest confidence in them.

The canoe was almost against the bank, where something of the bewilderment of Ashman seemed to enter the head of Bippo. He spoke to his companions and the three ceased paddling. Ashman had done so a moment before and was scanning the bank with a searching but vain scrutiny.

"You must have been mistaken," he said in a low voice; "they could not have swam the river and they had no other way of crossing."

"We seed 'em—motion dat way," and the native beckoned with his right arm, just as a person would do when signaling another to approach.

"I can't understand it," replied Ashman, with a shake of his head.

His doubts were confirmed, when he recalled that the professor and Jared Long had gone up the bank of the river with the purpose of learning the extent of the rapids. It followed, therefore, that if they had made their way to the other shore, it must have been at a point so far above the angry waters that there was no danger of being caught in the furious current.

He was turning over these troublous thoughts, when Bippo, who was facing the bank they had left, uttered an expression of dismay and extended his arm toward the shore behind them.

Ashman turned his head, and there in the moonlight he saw Professor Grimcke and the New Englander standing on the land and motioning to them to return.

Edward S. Ellis

"Yes—dat de way he do—he move arm like *dat*," said Bippo; "we hurry to go to him, den he ain't here—but *dere*."

Ashman could not doubt that the servant believed the extraordinary assertion he had just made, and such being the case, the startling truth was manifest; they had seen two strangers whom they mistook for their own friends, and these strangers had beckoned them to paddle the canoe to the other shore where they were awaiting them.

If such were the fact—and he did not doubt it—a new mystery confronted him.

Who were the white men and strangers? and why had they disappeared when approached by the canoe and its occupants?

Ashman ordered the servants to turn the craft about and return to the shore they had left with all speed. While doing so, and while Grimcke and Long were doubtless wondering what had got into the heads of the others, the young man wrought himself into a most uncomfortable condition of mind.

He questioned Bippo more particularly as to the appearance and actions of the strangers. It was clear that he, as well as the other two, still believed the couple on the opposite bank were Grimcke and Long; though when reminded that it was impossible that they could have crossed and recrossed the stream in such a brief time, and without any means except that of swimming, they only shook their heads, signifying that, though they could not explain *that* feature of the strange business, they would not yield their belief.

Ashman asked further, directing his question to each of the natives in turn, whether they saw the parties plainly enough to make sure they were white men. The servants were positive on this point, adding the distracting statement that they were dressed precisely like the two absent members of the little company, and that each carried a rifle as they did.

"Same ones—same ones; don't know how cross riber, but allee same do so," repeated Bippo, with a grin.

By this time the swiftly moving canoe was well on the way to the camp which it had left so abruptly, and, a minute later, Ashman sprang out and grasped the hand of each of his friends in turn.

In a few words he explained the extraordinary incidents of the last half hour, receiving in return the story of the experience of the Professor and his companion. The latter were deeply touched by the loss of Johnston. Danger tends to draw the members of a party closely together, and, despite the peculiar disposition of the sailor, the three felt a deep attachment for him. They would have faced any danger in his behalf, but the time had passed for that, and they could only mourn the loss of such a valuable comrade.

"But what about this story that Bippo tells?"

Before a reply could be made, the native approached, with his peculiar grin.

"How you cross riber?—why you come back 'gin? Why you no stay ober dere when we hurry to go to you?"

"Bippo, you are mistaken," replied the Professor, with all the earnestness at his command. "We went up this side of the stream, and have not been on the other side since dark. When we came back and saw that you were not in the camp, we thought you had all been killed."

Edward S. Ellis

The native grinned more than ever, and shook his head.

"De Purfes'r funny man—he make laugh." And he walked back to his companions with an unshakeable belief in the story given to Fred Ashman when he dashed in such excitement from the wood.

"Bippo believes what he has told us," said Long, who had studied the fellow closely; "and it follows that he and the others *did* see a couple of white men."

"I imagined," remarked Grimcke with something like regret in his tones, "that we were the first of our race to reach this spot; but it is hard in these days to find any place on the globe where some white person had not been before us."

"If there are a couple of them over there," said Ashman, scanning the opposite bank, "they ought to be friends; and, after signaling to our servants to cross, it is inexplainable that they should withdraw from sight as they did."

"We can depend on *one* thing," added the Professor; "we haven't seen the last of them. I would be glad to believe them friends, but their actions are unsatisfactory. I am inclined to think that the cause of their withdrawing was your entrance into the canoe. For some reason they wished to have nothing to do with any of us."

"It may be that since we are suspicious of them," said Fred, "they feel the same toward us, and are unwilling to make our acquaintance until after reconnoiterin' us. Helloa! what's up now?"

This question was caused by the action of Bippo, who, trembling in every limb, and with the appearance of a person overcome with terror, pointed to the forest behind them.

CHAPTER IX

A NATIVE HERCULES

The savages that had shown such pluck in the instances described, now gave another striking proof of their courage.

At the moment the mystified explorers were discussing the strange appearance and actions of the white men, more than twenty of the athletic barbarians issued as stealthily as phantoms from the trail leading from the forest and crouched along the edge of the timber.

Their silence added impressiveness to the singular scene and prevented their movements being observed except by Bippo, who was so terrified that he could only tremble and point at them.

They were partly hidden by the shadow which put out a short distance from the fringe of the wood, but there could be no doubt of their hostile intentions. They assumed the form of a line, somewhat after the manner of the combatants in the square of the native village. This was to give free play to their arms in flinging their javelins.

The occasion was one in which the fate of the explorers depended upon their promptness and bravery. Anything like

54 Edward S. Ellis

timidity or hesitation meant sure destruction, and the whites knew it.

"Into the boat!" commanded Ashman, addressing Bippo and his friends.

The words were like an electric shock to the helpers, who instantly clambered into the canoe and lay flat behind the luggage, where they were safe from the poisoned missiles that would soon be flying through the air.

Those natives, with their crude weapons, were only incumbrances in a crisis like the present.

The whites exchanged but a word or two and then opened the ball.

A savage, evidently the leader, and one who probably now saw the whites for the first time, had the audacity to step forward a couple of paces, and with a yell of defiance, raised his spear over his head.

Before he could launch the missile Jared Long sent a bullet through him, and then, shifting the muzzle of his Winchester toward the line of dusky figures, he blazed away as fast as he could sight the weapon and pull the trigger.

At the same instant the Professor and Ashman opened, and the bombardment which followed was enough to strike terror to the hearts of a hundred men.

It was more than the savages could stand, but, great as was their panic, most of them hurled one or two javelins apiece at the white men who stood fearlessly erect and combated them. They had come from their village prepared for a fight, and each warrior was provided with several of the poisoned missiles.

Before the explorers had emptied the magazines of their Winchesters not a live foe was left. The affrighted survivors, shrieking with terror, scrambled hastily back among the trees, some of them dragging the dead bodies, so that the spot was freed of the dusky miscreants with as much suddenness as it had been occupied by them.

There were plenty of shots left, and, after the disappearance of the savages, the whites fired into the woods, where they had vanished, not with the expectation of accomplishing anything more than adding to the panic.

When it was sure the wretches were gone, our friends made their preparations for leaving the spot, for nothing was clearer than that such was the wisest step to take.

It will be borne in mind that all the trouble had taken place on the left bank of the Xingu, no savages having been observed on the western bank. The daring of the savages could not be questioned. They had faced death repeatedly, and now, that they had the strongest of all motives— revenge—to prompt them, they were sure to use every means possible to bring about the ruin of the whites and their three native companions.

The forest, extending so close to the river, was a constant menace, for it afforded the best kind of shelter. Indeed, had the savages been less courageous and kept among the trees, taking a stealthy shot as the chance offered, they would have had a much better chance of doing what they wished and with less risk to themselves.

The javelins flung in blind desperation went wide of their mark, with the exception of one which whizzed over the canoe within a few inches of Bippo's head. The fellow was peeping furtively above the luggage, and heard the whizz of the missile passing fearfully close. He instantly ducked with such emphasis that he almost broke his nose against the bottom of the craft.

Striking the water beyond, the spear sank as abruptly as if it were a cannon ball.

The belief of our friends was that the troublesome natives were entirely confined to the left bank, though it was not likely they refrained from crossing so narrow a stream as the Xingu at its upper portion.

If the savages had been slow to learn from their first experience with the white men, there could be no doubt that the valuable lesson of the last encounter would not be lost upon them. The space between the edge of the wood and the margin of the river was so slight that it was the easiest thing in the world for one of them to launch his javelin with terrific force across it, and they would do so before morning, if the chance were given them.

If the other bank were reached, the savages would be easily detected in the bright moonlight, if they attempted to swim across or used some of their own boats. The only way in which they could avoid detection would be by crossing above or below this point.

They would hardly ascend the Xingu for this purpose, since the rapids would oblige them to travel a long way, and the place of ferryage, therefore, was likely to be below the campfire.

Such were the views of the whites, as they shoved the canoe into the stream, and stepping within, seized the paddles, which the helpers were too frightened to use effectively, while so near the dreaded shore.

Fred Ashman had taken but a few strokes when he handed the implement to Bippo and ordered him to use it. Then, resuming his Winchester, he faced the land, half suspecting they would not be allowed to reach the other side without some demonstration on the part of their fierce antagonists.

Time was of the first importance, and all the paddles in the craft were plied with the utmost possible vigor, each yard passed adding to the hope that hostilities were over for the time.

Probably three-fourths of the distance was accomplished, when a low exclamation from Ashman caused all to cease paddling and gaze at the shore which he was watching with such interest.

The most gigantic savage yet seen had emerged from the forest trail, but instead of advancing to the river's edge, he halted just far enough from the wood to allow the moonlight to inclose him. He was thus in almost as plain-sight as if it were mid-day.

He stood in silent contemplation of the strangers that had invaded his dominions and given his people such a dear lesson. Confident that he could accomplish no harm, even if he wished to try it, Ashman refrained from firing, while the company surveyed him with a feeling akin to admiration.

He was over six feet in height and of massive proportions. He would have been an ugly customer in a tussle where the conditions were equal, and Ashman could not forbear the thought that he was one of the contestants in the frightful sport he had witnessed near the village. If so, there was little doubt that he was hailed the champion. It may have been that he had hastened along the forest path, burning with a desire to assail the mysterious beings who had used his countrymen so ill, and he was filled with chagrin and disappointment that he had arrived too late.

But there was no end to the fancies that might be formed concerning him. That there was little imagination about Bippo was shown by his timid request to his masters to shoot the savage. To Bippo the elimination of a single enemy of such formidable mien was a consummation devoutly to be prayed for. But the Professor reminded the native that they only slew in self-defense.

All at once, the herculean savage was seen to make a motion of his arm, and before the act could be understood, the terrified Bippo called out that he was about to throw his javelin. At the same instant he and his two companions cowered in the bottom of the boat, where they were abundantly protected.

"The poor fellow is disappointed," laughed Ashman, "and he must show his anger, even if it requires the loss of one of his—"

Something like the flitting of a bird's wing whisked so close to the speaker's face that he involuntarily threw back his head. At the same instant, a heavy javelin crashed through the side of the boat, as if it were cardboard, and splashed out of sight in the water beyond.

The missile of the gigantic savage had passed between Ashman and the Professor, missing both by a few inches.

The young man, like a flash, brought his rifle to his shoulder and sighted at the savage who was still in plain sight, as if defying the whites to do their worst.

But Ashman did not pull the trigger. Lowering his weapon, he said:

"You have earned your life."

Edward S. Ellis

CHAPTER X

DOUBLE-GUARDED

The native who had made the wonderful throw of the javelin stood a moment longer, and then as if satisfied that he could do no more, he turned about and disappeared.

Fortunately, the missile had struck the upper part of the canoe, through which it tore a jagged hole several inches wide, and a short distance above the water. The injury could be easily repaired, and at present required no attention.

The paddles were again called into play, and the prow of the craft gently touched shore.

Having reached the right bank, the explorers had something to think of beside the savages whom they hoped were left behind for good. Two white men were known to be in the neighborhood, and there was warrant for believing they were as hostile as the natives from whom our friends had had such a narrow escape. With their superior intelligence, there was more to be feared from them than from the brave but ignorant savages; but, at the same time, it was to be hoped they might be conciliated, and that, if not, they would fight without the use of the fearful implements used by the savages, who held human life in such light esteem.

On the other hand, the explorers were too sensible to believe they had seen the last of the warriors that had proven their daring and ferocity.

It was decided to leave all the luggage in the canoe which was held so lightly against the bank that it could be shoved into the river at an instant's need. No fire was to be kindled, although the entire party left the boat and advanced to the edge of the wood, beneath whose shelter they seated themselves on the ground.

The night which they had hoped would afford them much needed rest, promised to be most exhausting in its requirements.

It had been the custom of the explorers, when camping on their way to the Matto Grosso, to have at all times a couple of their number on guard, the night being divided into two watches. For the first five hundred miles, after leaving the Amazon, this precaution was mainly to provide against the wild animals, that were always prowling around camp, and often showed a curiosity to make the acquaintance of the sleepers, and especially of their supplies.

The white men held an earnest consultation, while occupied in eating their evening meal or lunch. Had they deemed it prudent to kindle a fire, they would have prepared some fragrant coffee, of which they carried an abundance, though plenty of the little berries were encountered growing wild along the Xingu.

But that much-relished refreshment was now dispensed with, and they ate their fruit and a slight quantity of dried meat in darkness. The fish in the river was an unfailing source of supply, but that species of food also required fire in its preparation, and was therefore out of the question for

Edward S. Ellis

the time.

Their latitude was about fifteen degrees south, the temperature being so mild that the whites could have got along very well with as scanty raiment as their native helpers, though, as has been intimated, they clung to a civilized costume. They wore broad Panama hats, flannel shirts, with no coats or vests, and strong duck trousers thrust into their bootlegs. Thus attired, they were probably as comfortable as they could be.

A belt around the waist contained a supply of cartridges for their Winchesters and revolvers, besides affording a resting place for the knives, the indispensible Smith & Wesson being carried in the hip pocket, after the usual fashion.

In view of the unusual peril threatening the party, extra precautions were taken against surprise. It was arranged that Quincal and Jared Long should mount guard until midnight, when they would give way to Pedros and the professor. This would leave Bippo and Ashman free from any duty, their turn to come the following night.

Ashman, however, insisted on taking a part which was somewhat original in its nature. He was confident that if the savages found it impracticable to cross the Xingu in sight of the explorers, they would pass down stream and endeavor to do so, at a point where they could not be observed by those in camp.

He meant, therefore, to station himself so as to be able to detect such a movement. With his repeating rifle at command, he was sanguine of defeating the attempt, even though made by a score of enemies.

But for the peculiar contour of the banks on both sides, the whites could have done much better by simply paddling the canoe a quarter of a mile down the river and then hiding under the overhanging vegetation; but it has been explained that the Xingu, when its volume was swelled by rain, had swept the shores with such violence that they were bare for a dozen feet from the water.

Such a movement, therefore, would have to be made in the full light of the moon, and would, therefore, be plainly perceptible from the opposite bank—a fact which rendered the precaution of no avail.

All conceded the wisdom of Ashman's plan. The Professor urged him in case he found himself growing drowsy, to return at once to camp and allow one of his friends to take his place. The young man gave his promise, and, bidding them good-by, he began stealing down the stream, keeping as closely within the wall of shadow as he could, and advancing with as much care as though he saw the fierce savages across the Xingu watching for just such a movement.

The peculiar nature of the ground rendered progress easy, and he paused after going about a furlong, believing he had advanced sufficiently far to accomplish what he wished.

The essential work of Ashman was to cover one-half the distance between him and the camp, the further half being under the surveillance of the guards on duty there. Since he could also overlook the stream equally far in the opposite direction, it will be seen that the savages would have to make their crossing nearly a fourth of a mile below the camp to escape observation.

All this was on the theory that the lone sentinel was really able to scan the space with sufficient clearness to detect anything of the nature apprehended, and that the savages themselves had no suspicion of any such extra care on the part of their enemies.

The astonishing brilliancy of the moonlight will be appreciated, when it is stated that Ashman felt not the least doubt of his ability to meet every requirement of his self-assumed duty.

Well aware, from previous experience, of the insidious approach of slumber to the most vigilant sentinel, when unable to keep in motion, he avoided sitting down, even though he never felt more wakeful. So long as he stood erect, there was no danger of his lapsing into unconsciousness.

Another indispensable requirement was that he should not be tempted into venturing from the shadow where he stood, for such an act was liable to bring about discovery and defeat the very object that had brought him thither.

The moon was so nearly in the zenith that the shade from the edge of the forest did not project halfway across the open space to which we have alluded. It was in this partial gloom that the young man took his station, placing himself as far back as he could without standing among the trees themselves.

He was in the position of one who feels that the lives of his dearest friends are placed in his hands. To him, nothing was more evident than that the revengeful savages would attempt to cross the stream and make another stealthy attack upon the camp. They surely must feel enough dread of the terrible weapons that had wrought such havoc, not to defy them again, but would make their next demonstration in the nature of a flank movement.

One fact caused Ashman some surprise; he had seen nothing of any canoes or boats, which were plentiful along the shores of the Xingu below. It was not to be supposed that such a powerful and brave tribe as those on the other side, would live in a country abounding in streams, without finding need of such craft.

But because he had not seen them, was no proof that they were not in existence. They may have been drawn up among the trees, their precise location known only to their owners.

The prospect of holding his place for several hours, with his senses at a high tension, was not an inviting one, for he did not expect the savages to make their attempt before midnight; all such people aiming to surprise their enemies when wrapped in profound slumber.

But Ashman had not been at his station a half hour, when, to his amazement, he discovered that something was going on across the river directly opposite.

Despite the strong moonlight, he was unable to guess for a long time what it meant. He first heard a splash, as though a body had fallen or been thrown into the water, and then, for several minutes, everything was still as before.

It was a source of annoyance to him that at this moment, when he hoped to keep his attention fixed on matters on the other bank, he should be disturbed by a sound among the trees directly behind him. He, turned sharply and looked around, for the noise which had caught his attention was a footfall beyond all question.

But, if the youth was to be taken between two fires, he was ready. The stranger nearest him could have no thought of his proximity, or he would have taken more care to suppress any

Edward S. Ellis

noise. Since he was so much nearer than him on the other side. Ashman was forced to give his whole attention for the moment to the former's approach.

His suspense was brief, for while he stood with rifle ready, a large puma, or American lion, emerged from a point a couple of rods away, walked in his stealthy fashion to the edge of the river and began lapping the water.

Ashman wished nothing with him in view of more important business elsewhere, and he, therefore, stepped softly back in the wood, before the beast finished drinking.

The puma quickly slaked his thirst, and then, raising his head, looked about him with an inquiring stare as though he scented something suspicious. He gazed toward the other shore and finally swung himself lightly around, and trotted back to the forest.

Just before entering, he abruptly stopped and looked toward the spot where Ashman was concealed. He offered a tempting shot, but it hardly need be said that the young man restrained himself, and the next minute the beast vanished.

CHAPTER XI

A MYSTIFIED SENTINEL

Jared Long, the New Englander, and Quincal, the native helper, were the sentinels on duty in the immediate vicinity of the camp.

The professor was wearied from a hard day's work, and, feeling that everything possible had been done for the safety of all, stretched out upon his blanket on the soft ground and was soon asleep.

He expected to assume his duty as guardsman in the course of a few hours, and needed all the rest he could get before that time.

Bippo and Pedros were so disturbed by what they had witnessed, that, though they lay down at the same time, it was a good while before they closed their eyes in slumber. Their homes were near the mouth of the Xingu, and, even at that remote point, they had heard so many fearful accounts of the ferocious savages that infested the upper portions of the river, that they never would have dared to help in an attempt to explore the region but for the liberal pay promised, and their unbounded faith in the white men and their firearms.

Edward S. Ellis

The poor fellows would have given all they had, or expected to have, to be transported down the Xingu and out of the reach of the terrible natives who used their poisoned arrows and javelins with such effect; but, behold! the explorers, undaunted by what had taken place, had no thought of turning back, but were resolved to push on for an unknown distance, and Bippo and his friends had no choice but to go with them, for to run away would insure certain death at the hands of these people who seemed to be all around them.

Jared Long had so little faith in the usefulness of the servant Quincal as sentinel, that he arranged to place the least dependence possible on him. With no supposition that any danger was likely to come from the woods behind them, he sent the fellow a short distance back, instructing him to keep his ears and eyes open, since if he failed to do so, some wild animal was likely to devour him.

In crossing the Xingu below the falls, the rapid current had swept the canoe downward, so that it lay against the bank at a point fully two hundred yards below. It was here that the American stationed himself, standing, like Fred Ashman, just far enough from the water to be shrouded in the slight but increasing shadow made as the moon slowly worked over and beyond the zenith.

Looking across to the other shore, he could discern nothing upon which to hang a suspicion; but the first thing, perhaps trifling in itself, which attracted notice, was the unusual quantity of driftwood which appeared to be coming through the rapids and floating past.

As has been stated, in such a wooded country as the Matto Grasso there was always more or less of this, and Long had taken a critical survey of the rapids and noted the stuff which went plunging and dancing through them. Now, however, he was sure there was an increase, and a good deal of it consisted of large trees and logs, which must have been brought down by some cause more than ordinary.

Had there been anything else to occupy his attention, the fact would have escaped him, but the sentinel who is alive to his duty, notes little things, even when they seem to have no bearing on the great subject which engages all his energies.

It was a long way from the camp to the source of the Xingu, and in such a vast country as Brazil, there might have been a violent storm raging at that moment above and below them without the least evidence, so far as they could see, around them. Like all countries, that portion of empire is ravaged at times by fierce hurricanes and cyclones, which might have uprooted scores of trees and flung them into the waters which were now bearing them toward the Amazon and the broad Atlantic.

The sentinel naturally gave his chief attention to the other side of the Xingu, where so many stirring scenes had taken place that afternoon and evening. The camp-fire, which had been left burning, had smouldered so low that none of the embers were discernible, and only a thin column of smoke crept slowly upward marking where it had been. But this vapor was so clearly seen in the wonderful moonlight that it was easy to fix the precise point where the trail entered the wilderness.

It was just there, as Long believed, that the savages would debouch into sight, and renew the warfare which thus far had been only one series of disasters to them.

He was not mistaken, when, shortly after he had noticed the increasing number of logs and driftwood, he fancied he detected something going on at the very point on which his gaze was fixed.

As was the case with Fred Ashman, it was some time before he could so much as conjecture its nature. The glimpses were so faint and momentary that nothing tangible resulted, though he was positive that some of their enemies were there.

At the moment he uttered an exclamation of impatience, he made out three figures of the natives, who advanced far enough from the wood for him to identify them.

Not only that, but they walked stealthily to the edge of the river and stood several minutes, as if looking across at the canoe.

Long was confident that he could drop one of them at least, and he was tempted to do so. The most effective way of keeping the savages off was by nipping their schemes in the bud, and filling them with additional terror of the white strangers.

But he decided to wait a while, suspecting, as he did, that some scheme whose nature he could not guess was under way, and that if the projectors were undisturbed, it would soon be revealed.

Jared Long, we say, was convinced that the natives were scrutinizing the canoe and seeking to learn something about the occupants, whom they had doubtless watched as they made their way from the water to the shelter of the wood. Such was his belief, and yet he was altogether mistaken.

It struck him as odd that the savages acted as they did, when it would seem that they could see just as well from the edge of the wood, where they were not exposed to the fire of their enemies; but he reflected that there was precious little about the conduct of the natives from the first that could be explained on the line of common sense and consistency.

The trio stood in view less than five minutes, when they darted back to cover, as if afraid of being seen by the whites, a theory altogether untenable under the circumstances.

The natural supposition of the sentinel was that a large number of the savages had gathered under the bank and were making ready for some demonstration, which would soon take place.

It was not yet time to awaken the Professor and the natives. In fact, the plucky New Englander half believed that with his repeating rifle he would be able to beat off any approach from the other shore.

At this moment, he was amazed to see one of the savages do an extraordinary thing.

Darting out from the wood behind him, he ran to the smouldering camp-fire seized a brand that was covered with ashes, and circled it so swiftly about his head that it was fanned into a roaring blaze.

While doing this, he stood apparently with one foot in the margin of the Xingu, and evidently with not the slightest fear of the white strangers within gun-shot. He not only swung the brand forward several times, but reversed and spun it in the other direction, with a velocity that made it look like a solid ring of fire.

Suddenly the truth flashed upon the bewildered sentinel: *the savage was signaling to some friend or friends on the other bank*! That being the case, it followed that the friend or friends were most uncomfortably close to the camp of the white men.

And still Long failed to attach any importance to the unusual quantity of logs and driftwood that was sweeping down the Xingu in front of him.

CHAPTER XII

TO THE DEATH

It was at this juncture that Jared Long, peering out from the shadow of the wood, observed a larger log than any he had yet noticed, sweeping by within a short distance of shore.

It was without any branches, except a few near the top, but there seemed to be a number of big knots projecting from the upper side. He counted seven and they were all of the same size. Furthermore, unless he was mistaken, the huge tree, from some cause, was working closer to land.

Suddenly one of the knots moved!

The sentinel uttered an exclamation, for the startling truth flashed upon him with the quickness of lightning.

Each apparent knot was the head of a native!

With amazing coolness, the New Englander brought his Winchester to a level, and *bang, bang, bang*, he shattered three of the knots in quick succession.

He would not have stopped the frightful work even then, had not the other targets disappeared.

Awaking to their danger, the warriors, dropped down so low in the water that the log intervened between them and the deadly marksman.

Still the tree with its terrible load was approaching land. The natives were swimming toward shore and pushing it in front of them.

Long stepped back and roused the professor, placing his mouth so close to his ear that he was able to apprise him of what was going on, without being heard by their enemies.

Grimcke bounded to his feet, rifle in hand.

"We'll take them as they come out!" he replied, instantly grasping the situation.

The log was drifting lower down at the same time that it neared the land. Determined to confront the savages the instant they came forth, the explorers hurried along the edge of the wood, so as to be on the spot when the landing should be made. It was well they did so, for a more astounding discovery than the first, instantly followed the movement.

More than one of the trees that had floated by carried its human freight, and nearly a score of savages were crouching in the edge of the river, so flat on their faces that not one was visible from the spot where the sentinel was standing a moment before.

The natives, with a cunning that was never suspected, had crossed the Xingu above the rapids, where, as they knew, such a proceeding would not be anticipated by the explorers. Then, stealthily making their way to the bottom of the rapids, they first launched a number of trees and logs until, as may be said, the white man on guard should become so accustomed to them that they would cause no distrust.

If he should be tempted to scrutinize the first, he would learn that nothing was amiss and would let the rest go by unquestioned.

As a result, the natives had floated past the canoe and under the very nose of the sentinel without his detecting it.

The savage who swung the torch on the other side of the river probably meant it as a command for the daring raiders to make no further delay in their attack.

The group lying against the shore must have been puzzled by the sudden bombardment from the edge of the wood. They were so disconcerted, that instead of springing to their feet and charging upon the two defenders of the camp, half of them turned about, and diving deep into the stream, began furiously swimming for the other shore.

They must have concluded that there was a hitch somewhere in the programme, and the time for disappearing had arrived.

The other half, however, leaped to their feet, and, brandishing their spears and yelling at the top of their voices, ran swiftly in the direction of the whites, who were still firing their Winchesters.

"Get behind a tree!" shouted the professor, who had a wholesome dread of the poisoned weapons, and who lost no time in availing himself of the nearest shelter.

But he did not cease to use his rifle. The cartridges in his magazine were running low, and it was necessary to exercise care in aiming, for a few precious seconds must be consumed in extracting an additional supply from the belt at his waist.

Edward S. Ellis

But Jared Long declined to follow the sensible advice and example of his friend. Scorning to seek shelter, even from such terrible weapons, he blazed away, making nearly every shot tell.

It was not until he saw a knot of savages working round with a view of getting behind him, that he fell back a few paces, though still exposed. The wonder was that he had not already been pierced by more than one of the fatal missiles.

Suddenly he was jerked almost off his feet. The impatient professor had seized his arm and yanked him behind the tree at his side in spite of himself.

The New Englander would have been a zany to expose himself again, after being provided in this summary fashion with a shield.

But he, too, had about emptied the magazine of his Winchester. Although he could have brought out more cartridges from his belt in a twinkling, he coolly leaned his rifle against the tree and whipped out his revolver.

"After that is emptied," he reflected, "my knife is left."

The action of the natives suggested that it was their wish to take both the men prisoners instead of killing them. They had done too much to be let off with such an easy death: they were wanted for torture.

But, in making such a contract, it may be said that the assailants found it exceedingly difficult to deliver the goods.

They might as well have tried to seize and hold a couple of diminutive volcanoes, as to lay hands on the men whose supply of fire and death seemed without limit.

In the midst of the frightful struggle, with the shrieking figures falling, dashing forward and retreating, as if in wild bewilderment, Quincal rushed out of the wood with a shout brandishing his spear and making straight for the ferocious savages.

With a daring and strength that surprised the latter no more than it did his white friends, he drove the head of the weapon sheer through one of the assailants, who went over backward with a screech that drowned all other noises.

Quincal still grasped his weapon with both hands, and with amazing power, extricated it, as his victim fell, and turned upon the others.

But, by this time, he was surrounded and his fate was sealed.

Anxious to save the brave fellow, the professor and Long emptied their revolvers among his enemies, but were unable to scatter them until the fellow sank to the ground, pierced deep and fatally in a dozen places by the poisoned javelins.

Instinctively, the two white men filled their magazines from their belts, as quickly as they could, and by the time Quincal was no more, they opened again on the savages.

The latter had already lost fearfully, and this renewed assault was more than they could stand. If, instead of trying to make the white men prisoners, they had contented themselves with hurling their spears, when they first sprang from the ground, nothing could have saved Grimcke and Long.

Now, when they launched the missiles, it was too late. The white men were each protected by the trunk of a large tree, and standing back in the shadow, their faces could not be seen. The only way of locating them was by the flash of their guns.

They sent a shower of the javelins into the wood, and then were seized with that strange, aimless panic which sometimes comes over the bravest men in the crisis of a conflict. The survivors made a wild break for the river, into which they sprang as far as they could leap, diving deep, swimming as far as possible beneath the surface, then coming up an instant for breath and diving again.

The blood of the Professor and the American was at fever heat. They felt it wrong to show mercy, after what had taken place, and were in no mood for any further weakness of that nature.

Both ran down to the edge of the stream, and, standing almost in the water, took deliberate aim at every black head as it rose to the surface. They kept popping up here and there, at varying distances, only to drop out of sight again, the instant the swimmer caught breath; but in many instances, when they went down the second or third time, they did not come up again.

Professor Grimcke and Jared Long were throwing away no ammunition.

Finally, the dark forms began rising from the river on the other shore, where they darted into the wood, fearful of the dreadful messengers which followed them even there.

The repulse was decisive and there was little fear of the attack on the camp being renewed that night.

The shocking evidences of the disastrous repulse were on

every hand, with the body of poor Quincal lying at the feet of the assailant whom he had slain, and with nearly a score of dusky bodies stretched in every conceivable attitude.

Edward S. Ellis

CHAPTER XIII

A CHANGE OF CAMP

Professor Grimcke and Jared Long stood like a couple of warriors, exhausted from the desperate conflict which they had been waging for hours.

And yet the sanguinary contest had lasted but a few minutes, while they who had wrought all this destruction did little more than stand, aim and fire their guns. The task of the natives was tenfold harder, as the results were tenfold worse against them.

Like old hunters, the first thing the explorers did was to fill the magazines of their Winchesters with cartridges, after which their revolvers were reloaded. Then they were ready for business again.

At this moment, Bippo and Pedros crept from the wood, the picture of quaking terror. They had been roused at the beginning of the tumult, but deeming discretion the better part of valor, scrambled farther back into the forest, where they remained almost dead with fright, until sure the awful scene was over.

There can be little question that Quincal was as much

terrified as they and possibly more. It was his very excess of panic, which turned his head, and caused him to do that which would have been beyond his power under other circumstances.

When they saw the dead body of their comrade, Bippo and Pedros broke into loud lamentations. There could be no doubt that they mourned the poor fellow as much as did the explorers who had witnessed his death.

The surroundings of the camp were so frightful that the Professor proposed they should get beyond sight of it by drifting further down stream, a proposal to which his companion willingly agreed.

What should be done with the body of Quincal? This was the question which caused the party to hesitate a minute or two after the canoe was shoved into the water and ready to float down stream.

The wishes of his companions were asked, and Bippo replied that the most fitting burial, and one in accordance with the peculiar customs of their people, was to give it burial in the Xingu.

This was in consonance with the feelings of Grimcke and Long, and they at once made arrangements to carry out the plan.

The remains were tenderly carried into the boat, and a large stone fastened by means of a piece of rope to the ankles, which were tied together. Then the craft was paddled to the middle of the river, and the body carefully lifted over the side. Holding it thus suspended for a minute or two, Jared Long and the Professor lifted their hats and closed their eyes while the New Englander uttered a brief prayer, committing the soul to Him who gave it, commending the other body, lying alone in the dark forest where it had fallen, to the same merciful Father, and beseeching his protection to the living through the perils by which they were environed. A splash followed, and all that was mortal of the native sank out of sight to sleep until awakened by the trump of the resurrection morn.

The sad duty completed, the attention of the party was given to the duties before them.

It was a sorrowful reflection, that, since the set of sun, two of their number had yielded up their lives, and they had barely reached the edge of the Matto Grosso, that land of mystery into which they hoped to penetrate far enough to learn much that was yet unknown to the civilized world.

If they were compelled to pay such fearful toll before they were fairly within the strange region, what was to be the cost of exploring the wild country itself?

But while Bippo and Pedros were more anxious than ever to leave the section with its dreadful memories behind them, neither dare give expression to his thoughts, and the German and American were not made of the stuff which yields when first exposed to the fire.

They reasoned that if there were no such formidable difficulties to overcome, others would have visited the country long before and explored it so fully that nothing would be left for those who came after them. The prize is the most valuable for which the highest price is exacted. Neither referred to the abandonment of their work, for no such idea entered their minds.

It is not to be supposed that during the fearful scenes through which the leader of the expedition and his friend passed, they forgot that their friend Fred Ashman was only a short distance away. Indeed, one cause for pushing the canoe into the stream and allowing it to drift with the swift current was that they might join Fred with the announcement of what had taken place during his absence.

They supposed that he must have heard the rifle reports and the yells and shrieks of the natives during the desperate conflict, for though the rapids gave out a roar which penetrated miles, yet the sharp discharges and cries of the combatants were of a nature to be heard still farther.

Had the explorers suspected what was coming, Ashman, of course, would have staid with his friends; for his services were almost indispensable. In fact, but for the singular attempt of the natives to make captives of the white men, they would have been unable to withstand the terrific onslaught, despite the vast superiority of their weapons over those of the assailants.

It never occurred to Grimcke or Long that their friend could have got into trouble himself. He was removed from the scene of conflict, which was over so quickly that he could not have reached the spot in time to take part, had he started on the instant the first gun was fired.

But it struck both, while drifting downward and carefully scanning the shore, as strange that nothing had been seen of Ashman. Enough time had now elapsed for him to traverse the intervening distance several times, and it was to be supposed that he would have put in an appearance without delay, provided he was free to do so.

The two talked together in low tones, and admitted that there was something to cause misgiving in Fred's continued

Edward S. Ellis

absence. What could be the explanation?

The Professor was inclined to think their friend had gone farther down stream than he first intended; but, even if such were the fact, he hardly could have traveled so far that he would not have been well on his way back to the battle ground by this time.

The trend of the Xingu was such at this point, that the thin line of shadow along the wood on their left, as they passed down the river, steadily widened until it now almost reached the water itself. In a short time it would extend over the surface and afford the canoe that shelter which, had it come earlier in the evening, might have postponed the desperate conflict with the savages.

The move from above was merely to get away from the sights that met them at every turn; and, without seeking to drift to the point where Ashman was supposed to be waiting, the explorers turned the prow to land, which they touched a moment later.

It would have been more cheerful to have had a fire burning, but there was no other call for it. The mild temperature rendered it really more enjoyable without it, since the blaze was always sure to attract innumerable insects, and possibly might tempt the defeated natives to another effort to wipe out the deadly insults that had been theirs from the beginning.

It was not yet midnight, nor indeed anywhere near it, but the Professor volunteered to take his turn with Bippo for the remaining hours of darkness. But no such arrangement was necessary, since every member of the party was rendered wakeful by the exciting incidents, while the grief of Bippo and Pedros over the loss of their friend was sure to drive away all slumber for a long time.

The luggage was left in the canoe, where all the party would have stayed, had not their positions been so cramped as to render sleeping difficult. Their blankets were spread on the ground, where they reclined, talking in low tones, watching, listening, and speculating as to the cause of Fred Ashman's continued absence.

Long was about to open his mouth to advance a new theory, when a slight sound apprised him that either the young man they were talking about, or some one else, was approaching.

Edward S. Ellis

CHAPTER XIV

A STRANGE ENCOUNTER

Fred Ashman was standing near the edge of the Xingu, as will be remembered, when his attention was diverted for the moment by a puma, which came out of the wood, drank from the stream, and then, after a brief pause, returned to his shelter.

All this while, the dull roar of the rapids was in the explorer's ears, and he was eager to withdraw his attention from the beast and direct it upon the opposite shore, where he was convinced something unusual was going on.

The minute the beast disappeared, he looked across at the point that had so interested him.

The question which he had asked himself some time before, was answered by the sight of a small canoe that was stealing down the river, instead of heading directly across to where he was standing. In this boat was a single individual, using a paddle with the deftness of an American Indian.

Here was something that needed attention, and, with the aid of the brilliant moonlight. Ashman watched the craft and its occupant as closely as if his own fate were wrapped up in its movements—a supposition which it was not improbable was fact itself.

The savage moved slowly, as if sensible of the call for the utmost care, went only a few rods down stream, when he turned out in the water and aimed for the shore where the watcher was standing. He had gone some distance below, and it was to be supposed that the force of the current would carry him still farther, so that if he made a landing it was likely to be far below.

But he who held the paddle was a master of that species of navigation, and Ashman was surprised to observe that he was aiming at the very spot where he was standing carefully concealed in the shadow. If nothing interfered, they were sure of making a closer acquaintance.

The boat was about the middle of the river, when the white man was struck by the immense size of the occupant. He was one of the largest men he had ever seen, his weight sinking the canoe almost to its gunwales.

"He must be the savage who hurled his javelin through our boat," was the conclusion of the astonished Fred. "What a magnificent fellow he is!"

The native sat so that his face was turned toward the young man, who studied his countenance with the deepest interest.

He had the busy head, the large protruding eyes, and the dark, naked skin of all his people. His enormous arms swung the paddle first on one side of the boat and then on the other. As he did so, Fred saw the play of the splendid muscle, which was like that of Hercules himself. Rash would be that antagonist who engaged him in a hand-to-hand struggle.

Edward S. Ellis

Nothing in the world was easier than for the explorer to extinguish the life in that impressive specimen of physical manhood, without the least risk to himself, and yet, although he knew him to be the most formidable enemy of his people, he held no thought of doing him harm—at least not at the present stage of his extraordinary business.

It was at this decidedly interesting juncture that a new element obtruded itself. The sounds of guns, shouts and yells, in the direction of the rapids left no doubt that his friends there were having a lively time with the natives.

Ashman would have turned and made all haste thither, but for the presence of this burly giant in front. Whatever was going on down stream was with the full knowledge of him, and he was the one for the white man to look after.

Had the latter been surprised by the sounds of conflict, he would have ceased paddling or headed his boat up stream, but he merely glanced toward the rapids, and continued dipping his paddle and propelling his craft, as if it was his intention to step ashore and grasp the hand of the astonished youth awaiting his arrival.

The passage occupied but a very few minutes. Just before the bank was reached, he made one powerful sweep of the oar, which sent the prow far up the shingle, and then leaped as lightly as a cat from the structure, which bounded up as if relieved of several hundred pounds' weight.

Turning about, the giant stooped down and took a spear as long and heavy as the one he had hurled nearly across the Xingu, through the boat of the explorers.

It seemed that there was to be no end to the obtrusion of "side issues" upon the little drama going on under Fred

Ashman's eyes. It must have been that the puma which had slaked its thirst at the Xingu's margin a short time before, had become convinced that parties were near, entitled to his attention.

While endeavoring to locate him, he probably caught sight of the approaching native and concluded that he was the individual to whom he should turn.

Be that as it may, the native had only time to pick up his ponderous spear and face toward the wood, when the lion emerged from the broadening band of shadow, and, with a low, threatening growl, advanced upon him.

Like the cat species to which he belonged, he crouched so low while walking, that his shoulders protruded above his back in large humps, and his belly almost touched the ground. His long tail flirted angrily from side to side, his jaws were parted, disclosing his sharp, carnivorous teeth and blood-red tongue, while his eyes emitted a phosphorescent glow that was like fire itself.

He was a formidable antagonist, and as Ashman observed his movements and ugly appearance, he felt like pumping a half dozen bullets into his lank, muscular body.

But he experienced the natural interest of a sportsman in an impending fight, and was curious to see how the huge native would acquit himself in the struggle at hand.

He was not kept long in doubt. The savage observed the puma the moment his head emerged from the shadow into the moonlight, and he instantly prepared himself to meet him.

Little preparation, however, was necessary, for he carried but

Edward S. Ellis

the single weapon and that had only to be grasped in his right hand.

The warrior might have leaped into his craft and escaped by paddling out in the river, where he could drive the boat at a faster pace than the beast could swim, but he did nothing of the kind.

He neither advanced nor retreated, but, standing just in front of the prow, he rested on his right leg; with the left foot thrown forward, and the tremendous javelin balanced over his right shoulder.

His pose was admirable, and even in that thrilling moment compelled the admiration of the single spectator, who was strongly of the opinion that the puma, to put it mildly, was committing an error of judgment.

There may have been some strange, instinctive knowledge which penetrated the brain of the beast before he reached the assailing point, and which compelled him to stop. The individual whom he had selected as his victim was not to be crushed at a single effort, as he was accustomed to bring down the llamas, antelope, and other animals of the wilderness. No; there was something in that pose, the demeanor and the flash of the midnight eyes which forced the fierce creature to pause, when on the very death line, as it may be termed.

But if the native was defiant, the puma had no purpose of retreating from before such a powerful enemy. In his blind ferocity, he would have assailed him, could it have been impressed upon him that his own destruction would be the inevitable result.

The lank jaws were still parted and dripped foam, as the lion continued his cavernous growls, while his ears lying flat on his head in the manner peculiar to the feline species, the bristling spine and the lashing of the tail gave the beast the appearance of a bundle of concentrated fury, as indeed he was.

Fred Ashman was struck almost breathless by what followed.

He observed the curious, twitching movement of the puma's legs as they were gathered closer under his body, and which is always a sure evidence that the animal is about to make his decisive leap upon his victim. The native must have read the movement aright, for the hand over his shoulder was suddenly thrown back and instantly forward again, as his javelin left his grasp with terrific force and the suddenness of lightning.

But inconceivably quick as was the action, the puma dodged the missile, which entered the earth just behind him, and driven with such tremendous force was buried half its length in the ground.

Almost at the same instant the body of the lion rose in air and shot forward as if driven from the throat of a Parrott gun.

But if the brute was quick, so was the man, who dropped downward without moving his feet, and allowed his assailant to pass over his head and land directly in the canoe, where for a single second only he was partly hidden from sight.

Hardly had he landed, when the warrior darted forward several paces to where his javelin projected from the ground, seized it with both hands and wrenched it free. Whirling about, he confronted the beast once more, as he was gathering himself for a second leap.

The savage learned wisdom from what had just occurred, and instead of allowing the weapon to leave his hand, held it with an immovable grip and awaited the renewal of the attack.

The puma seemed also to have absorbed some instruction from his failure, and instead of leaping at once, began a stealthy advance, coming over the side of the canoe with the gliding motion of a serpent, and evidently wishing to get so near that his victim could not escape again by the means he used before.

Suddenly the native, still holding the javelin with both hands, stepped forward a single pace. This placed him in the strongest possible position, and, with one appalling thrust, he drove the spear for a distance of two feet into the chest of the puma, instantly snatching it forth again, moving back a couple of feet, and holding himself ready for any assault from the brute.

No need of any virus on the point of *that* weapon, for it had cloven the heart of the lion in twain, and he went down without a single groan, as dead as dead could be.

The native stepped to the river, washed the blood from the weapon and then turned about to resume his advance toward the wood.

As he did so, he found himself face to face with a white man, who, stepping from the shadow, held his Winchester leveled at him in an exceedingly suggestive fashion.

If Fred Ashman had been astonished before, what words shall describe his amazement when the dusky Hercules, calmly staring at him for a moment, said in unmistakable English, "*I surrender.*"

CHAPTER XV

ZIFFAK

Fred Ashman was so startled by hearing the giant native utter his submission in unmistakable English, that he came near dropping his leveled Winchester to the earth in sheer amazement.

He had not dreamed that the savage understood a word of that tongue, but judged from his own posture, with his weapon pointed at him, that the other knew when an enemy had "the drop" on him. Even if such were the fact, he counted upon a desperate resistance, and was prepared to give the fellow his quietus by a shot from his rifle.

The savage held his ponderous javelin in his hand, but made no effort to use it. His black eyes were fixed on the face of the handsome American, and he could not have failed to note the expression of bewilderment and wonder caused by the words that had just dropped from his dusky lips. Indeed, Ashman fancied he detected something akin to a smile lighting up the forbidding countenance.

It may be said that the young explorer for the moment felt himself in the position of the man who drew an elephant in a lottery—he didn't know what to do with his prize. It had

Edward S. Ellis

come to him so unexpectedly that he was bewildered.

But he was quick to rally from his dazed condition. The fact that the giant had shown such a knowledge of the English tongue suggested the possibility not only of obtaining important information, but of making a friend of this personage, who must possess great influence among his people.

True, the events of the afternoon and evening were against anything in the nature of comity or good will, but no harm could come from an attempt to bring about an understanding between the people and the explorers that had become involved in such fierce conflicts with them.

"Drop that spear!" commanded Ashman.

"I have surrendered," said the savage, in a low, coarse voice; "and Ziffak does not lie."

Nevertheless, while the words were passing his lips, he unclosed his right hand and allowed the implement to fall to the ground.

"Is your weapon poisoned?" asked Ashman, still mystified by the extraordinary situation and hardly knowing what to say.

"Your man in the wood was pierced by one of our spears; ask him."

"Such a warrior as Ziffak does not need to tip his weapons with poison," said Ashman, glancing significantly at the carcass of the puma. "It is cowardly to use such means against your enemies."

The savage shook his head and an ugly flash appeared in his eyes.

"Do not the whites from the Great River use fire to slay the natives before they can come nigh enough to use their spears?"

"But they have no wish to use them against your people; we would be their friends, and it pains us to do them harm; we would not have done so had they not compelled us."

Ziffak stood a moment as motionless as a statue, with his piercing black eyes fixed with burning intensity on the white man. The latter would have given much could he have read his thoughts, of which an intimation came with the first words that followed.

"Waggaman and Burkhardt told our people that if we allowed the white folks to come into our country, they would bring others and slay all our men, women and children."

"Who are Waggaman and Burkhardt?" asked the explorer, uncertain whether he was awake or dreaming.

"They have lived with the Murhapas for years; they are white men, but they are our friends."

Ashman recalled the story told by Bippo and his companions earlier in the evening. It must be that the names mentioned belonged to those two mysterious individuals, who beckoned them across the Xingu. For some reason of their own, they wished to keep all others of their race out of the country.

It was plain that Ziffak was a remarkable person and the explorer determined to use every effort to win his good will.

"Waggaman and Burkhardt have told you lies; we are your friends."

"Why do you not stay at home and leave us alone?"

"We expect to go back, after ascending the river a short distance further; nothing would persuade us to live here, and, as I have told you, we would not harm any person if they would leave us alone."

Ziffak seemed on the point of saying something, but checked himself and held his peace, meanwhile looking steadily at the man who had made him a prisoner in such clever style.

Ashman resolved on a rash proceeding.

"Take up your spear again, Ziffak; go back to your people, and, if you believe what I say, tell them my words, and ask them to give us a chance to prove that we mean all I have uttered."

"My people know nothing about you," was the strange response.

"You heard but a few minutes ago the sounds of guns and the shouts from the direction of the rapids, which show they were fighting."

"Those people are not mine," said the native; "but they are my friends, and I fight for them."

"From what you said, you are a Murhapa?"

Ziffak nodded his head in the affirmative.

"Where do they live?"

He extended his hand and pointed up the river.

"One day's ride above the rapids and you reach the villages of the Murhapas. There live Waggaman and Burkhardt; they came many years ago. I am a chieftain, and they rule with me."

"It was from them you learned to speak my tongue?"

Ziffak again nodded his head, adding:

"Many of my people speak it as well as I."

"Tell me, Ziffak, why, if your home is so far above the rapids, you are here among these people, whose name I do not know?"

"They are Aryks; they have much less people than the Murhapas, and are our slaves. Some days ago word was brought to us that a party of white men were making their way up the Xingu. Waggaman and Burkhardt and I set out to learn for ourselves and to stop them. They went down the other side of the river and I came down to the Aryk village. I roused them to kill you before you could pass above the rapids, but we were able to slay only one of them."

"And it was a sad mistake that you did that; for he was a good man, who wished you no evil. Where are Waggaman and Burkhardt?"

The native shook his head. He had picked up his spear, but made no movement toward taking his departure. Ashman hoped he would not, for everything said not only convinced him of the first importance of gaining the fellow's confidence, but encouraged him in the belief that he was fast doing so. He resolved to leave no stone unturned looking to that end.

"Why did not your two white friends help you in the fight, to keep us from going further up the Xingu?"

"*Maybe they did*," replied Ziffak, with a significant glance up stream, which left no doubt that he referred to the conflict that had taken place there while the couple were talking on the margin of the river.

"I don't believe it," Ashman hastened to say, hopeful that such was the case; for, with two white men and their firearms, the peril of his friends must have been greatly increased.

"Why do you seek to enter our country?" asked the dusky giant, after a brief pause.

"We want to learn about your people; but I pledge you we wish not to harm a hair of their heads."

It was not to be expected that a savage who has heard nothing else for years except that any penetration of his territory by white men meant destruction, could give up that belief simply on the pledge of one of the race accused.

But it was equally clear that this particular savage was favorably disposed toward Ashman. It may have been that his good will was won by the neat manner in which he had got the best of Ziffak, the most terrible warrior ever produced by that people. A brave man respects another brave man.

"Why did Waggaman and Burkhardt visit your villages and make their home with you for so many years?"

"I do not know," replied Ziffak, with another shake of his head; "but they have proven they are friends. They do not want to go back to their people, who are all bad."

The thought occurred to Ashman, though he did not express it, that the strange white men were criminals. They may have escaped from the diamond mines, which were at no great distance, and naturally preferred the free, wild life of the interior to the labor and tyranny which the miserable wretches condemned to service in those regions undergo.

"Ziffak," said the explorer, lowering his weapon, "will you walk back to the camp of my people? You have my promise that no harm shall be offered you by any one."

The herculean native nodded his head, and the strange couple started up the bank in the direction of the camp, which was now as silent as though not a hostile shot had been fired, or a savage blow been struck.

Edward S. Ellis

CHAPTER XVI

THE LAND OF THE MURHAPAS

It looked as if Fred Ashman had gained a double victory over the giant Ziffak, and his second triumph was infinitely greater than his first.

His heart thrilled at the thought that this formidable antagonist had been so suddenly transformed into a friend; and yet he could not entirely free himself from a certain misgiving, as the two walked side by side along the Xingu. Recalling the dexterity of the native—all the more wonderful because of his bulk—he reflected, that it was the easiest thing in the world for him to turn like a flash and pierce him with his poisoned javelin before the slightest defence could be made.

It was this thought which led him stealthily to place his hand on the butt of the revolver at his hip, prepared to whip it out and fire as quickly as he knew how. At the same time he edged away from him, so as to maintain considerable space between their bodies.

Ziffak suddenly changed his javelin from his right to his left hand, the movement sending a shock of fear through the American, who the next moment blushed from shame, for it was manifest that the shrewd savage suspected the timidity of his new friend, and shifted the frightful weapon to the side furthest from him to relieve any misgiving on his part.

The conversation continued as they walked, the native showing a surprising willingness to answer all questions.

Ashman gathered from what was told him that the Murhapas were a tribe numbering fully a thousand men, women and children; that they occupied a village or town on the right bank of the Xingu about twenty miles above the rapids, where the incidents already recorded occurred, and that they were far superior in intelligence, physical development and prowess to any other tribes in the Matto Grosso.

It was about five years before that the two white men, Waggaman and Burkhardt, suddenly made their appearance at the towns. The fact that they did not come up the Xingu, but from the forest to the south, strengthened Ashman's suspicion that they were criminals who had managed to escape from the Brazilian diamond mines, though it was a mystery how they had secured the two rifles which they brought with them. They had no revolvers, and their guns were not of the repeating pattern. When their ammunition gave out, one of them made a journey of several days' duration into the wilderness, invariably bringing back a supply which lasted a long time.

Such weapons were entirely unknown to the Murhapas, who had never heard of anything of the kind. The exploits of the owners caused the natives to look upon them with awe. They were soon established on the best of terms with their new associates, who allowed them to do as they chose in everything.

It is not to be supposed that Ashman gathered all the

information given in this chapter, during his brief walk with Ziffak. Indeed, that which has already been stated was obtained only in part during the memorable interview; but it may be as well to add other facts which afterwards came to the knowledge of him and the explorers, since it is necessary to know them in order to understand the strange series of incidents and adventures in which they became speedily involved.

The Murhapa tribe was ruled by King Haffgo, whose complexion was almost as fair as that of a European. He had fifty wives, but only one child, whose mother was dead. This child was a daughter, Ariel, of surpassing beauty and loveliness, the pride of her grim father and adored by all his subjects. From Waggaman and Burkhardt she had acquired a knowledge of the English tongue, which Ziffak declared was superior to his own. Both of these men had sought in turn to win her as his wife, and the king was not unwilling, because of the awe in which he held them; but Ariel would not agree to mate herself with either, though she once intimated that when she became older she might listen favorably to the suit of Waggaman, whose appearance and manner were less repulsive than those of his comrade.

The first duty the guests took upon themselves was to impress King Haffgo and his subjects that all white men except themselves were their deadliest enemies, and, if any of them were allowed to visit the village, they would assuredly bring others who would cause the utter destruction of the inhabitants.

Three years before, a party of six white explorers ascended the Xingu, and suddenly presented themselves to the Murhapas, without previous announcement or knowledge. Despite their professions of friendship, and a most valiant defence, they were set upon and slain the same hour they appeared among the fierce people.

Ariel, the daughter of the king, was but a child, at that time, just entering her teens. She did not know of the cruel massacre until it was over, when she surprised all by expressing her sorrow and declaring that a great wrong had been done the strangers. From that time forward, those who studied her closely saw that she had formed a strong distrust, if not dislike, of Waggaman and Burkhardt, though, seeing the high favor in which they were held in court, she sought to veil her true feelings.

Ziffak was a younger brother of the king, and bore the title of head-chieftain. He was next in authority and power, and, because of his immense size and prowess, led all expeditions against their enemies, none of whom was held in fear. Occasionally, he headed a hundred warriors, who made excursions through the neighboring wilderness and in pure wantoness spread destruction and death on every hand.

The Aryks, after receiving several such terrible visits, sued for terms and willingly agreed to consider themselves slaves of the Murhapas. Their location was favorable to detect the advance of any of the dreaded white men up the Xingu, and they agreed in consideration of being left alone, to check any such approach, a fact which will explain the fierceness and determination with which they contested the ascent of the river by our friends.

If they allowed the whites to pass above the rapids, they knew that the mighty Ziffak would sweep down upon them and visit frightful punishment upon their heads.

Instead of bringing a body of his own warriors, Ziffak, as has been intimated in another place, came alone down one side of the Xingu, with Waggaman and Burkhardt on the other, the calculation being to rouse enough Aryks to destroy the invaders, as they were regarded. Enough has been told to show how thoroughly the head-chieftain acquitted himself of this duty.

Several of the powerful reasons for the jealousy of Waggaman and Burkhardt of their race, was apparent in the fact that there was an astonishing abundance of diamonds and gold among the Murhapas. Although none was seen on Ziffak, it was only because he was on the war-path. He had enough at home to furnish a prince's ransom, while the possessions of the beautiful princess Ariel were worth a kingdom.

These were obtained from some place among the mountains to the westward of the town. In the same mysterious region was a peak, whose interior was a mass of fire that had burned from a date too remote to be known even in the legends of the wild people. There was a lake also, whose waters were so clear that a boat floating over them seemed suspended in mid air.

This wonderful section was claimed by King Haffgo, who would permit none but his subjects and the two white men to visit it. A party of Aryks; presuming upon the friendly relations just established with their masters, ventured to make their way to the enchanted place without permission or knowledge of the Murhapas.

Before they could get away, they were discovered by some of the lookouts, and every one slain with dreadful torture. The lesson was not lost upon their surviving friends, who never again ventured to repeat the experiment.

The Murhapas were the first to use the spears with the deadly points. They not only taught the Aryks how to prepare the poison from the venom of several species of serpents and noxious vegetables, but imparted to them the remedy,—a decoction of such marvellous power, that a single swallow would instantly neutralize the effect of any wound received from the dreaded missiles.

Among the tribes named, there was no knowledge of the use of iron though the ore is abundant in that region. The only objects composed of the metal were the firearms of the white men, and the natives could not comprehend how they were fashioned from the substance which underwent such a change from its native state.

Every implement used by this people is made from stone, which however seems almost the equal of iron and steel. Spear points, axes and cutting tools are shaped with remarkably keen edges, with which trees are readily felled, and cut into any form desired.

Shells are used in the formation of knives, while the teeth of certain fish, taken from the Xingu, enables them to construct still more delicate implements for cutting and carving.

Indian corn, cotton and tobacco are raised from a soil whose fertility cannot be surpassed, though strangely enough the tribes have no knowledge of the banana, sugar cane and rice, which belong so essentially to the torrid zones. Dogs and fowls are entirely unknown, and there is no conception of a God, though all have a firm belief that they will live again after death. A myth has existed among them from time immemorial of the creation of the world, which, according to their views, consists of the regions around the headwaters of the Xingu and Tapajos.

Ziffak was a favorite of the beauteous Ariel, and it is not improbable that, knowing as he did, her lamentation over the cruel death of the white men, who appeared at her home three years before, he was more willing than would otherwise have been the case to stay his hand, after doing such yeoman service against the new-comers.

Where these tribes came from is a question yet unsolved by anthropologists, though the theory has many supporters that most of the isolated peoples are allied to the original stock of the once mighty Caribs, who journeyed from the south to the sea.

Conscious of their own might, and knowing the prodigious mineral wealth at their command, the Murhapas are naturally jealous of their neighbors, and fight fiercely to resist anything that bears a resemblance to an encroachment upon their rights.

It will be understood that Waggaman and Burkhardt met with little difficulty in rousing their enmity particularly against the Caucasian race, since the members of that, of all others, were the ones most to be dreaded.

The foregoing, much of which is in the way of anticipation, we have deemed best to incorporate in this place.

CHAPTER XVII

THE NEW ALLY

The amazement which so nearly overwhelmed Fred Ashman during the few minutes succeeding the surrender of Ziffak, was shared in all its entirety, when the two presented themselves before the astounded explorers in the canoe.

In fact, Jared Long came within a hair of shooting the Hercules, before the situation could be explained to him. Even then he refused for awhile to believe the astonishing story, but declared that some infernal trickery was afoot. Finally, however, he and the Professor and Bippo and Pedros realized that the most powerful enemy had become their ally.

Ziffak showed a strange talkativeness after joining the company. Seating himself on the ground where all were now veiled in shadow, he answered the questions that were rained upon him, until most of the information given in the preceding chapter was told to the wondering listeners.

The account of the dreadful reception that awaited their predecessors three years before, would have deterred such brave men as the explorers from pushing further, but for the fact that they had secured an all-powerful friend at court. Believing that he could pave the way for a friendly reception, they were eager to visit what seemed to them an enchanted land.

There was some uneasiness over Waggaman and Burkhardt, who, it could be easily seen, would at the most do nothing more than disguise their enmity under the guise of friendship, holding themselves ready for some treachery that would bring about the death of the visitors.

The conversation lasted a long time, and was ended by the natural question put to Ziffak as to what should be the next step.

From what he had already stated, it was evident they were not yet through with the Aryks. Despite their frightful repulse, they would hold the Murhapas in greater dread than the whites; and, well aware of the penalty of allowing them to pass above the rapids, would never cease their efforts to prevent such a disaster. It followed, therefore, that something must be done to spike their guns, and Ziffak was the only one who could do it.

The whites were not surprised, when he offered to return to the point down the river, where he had left his canoe, recross to the other side, and make known to the Aryks that it was his wish that the explorers should be molested no further.

The announcement would be a surprise indeed to them, but there was none who would dare question the authority of such a source.

During the absorbingly interesting conversation, Ziffak stated that his object in coming from the other side was to reach the camp of the whites at the same time that an attack was made by the Aryks who so cunningly used the floating logs and trees as a screen to hide their approach. He preferred his course to that of accompanying them.

It will thus be seen, that, although the act of Fred Ashman in passing down the Xingu seemed like a mistake, yet it was the most providential thing that could have occurred.

Having made known his plan, the burly chieftain set about carrying it out with characteristic promptness. Without saying good-bye, he rose to his feet, and walking rapidly off, soon disappeared in the direction of the spot where took place his encounter with the puma and his meeting with Fred Ashman.

He had not been gone long, when those left in camp caught sight of the little boat skimming swiftly across the Xingu below them. The preliminaries of the singular movement in their favor was going on according to programme.

But, with the departure of Ziffak, something like a distrust of his friendship entered the minds of the three whites. Bippo and Pedros were so overcome by what they had seen that they were unable to comprehend what it all meant. They kept their places in the boat and listened and wondered in silence.

The Professor hoped for the best, though he admitted that there was something inexplainable in the business. He had spent hours in examining the strange fish of the Upper Xingu, in inspecting the remarkable plants, which he saw for the first time, and in studying the zoology and mineralogy of the region. He had been delighted and puzzled, over and over again, but all of these problems combined failed to astonish him as did the action of Ziffak and the story he told.

Ashman was the most hopeful of all. He had been with the native more than the rest, and was given the opportunity to study him closely. He was confident that he read the workings of his mind aright, and that the fellow would be their friend to the end.

Jared Long, the New Englander, was equally positive in the other direction. He maintained that since the leopard cannot change his spots, no savage showing such relentless hatred of the white race as did Ziffak, could be transformed into a friend for no other reason than that he had been made a prisoner.

He insisted further that, if he succeeded in helping them through to the Murhapa village, it would be only with the purpose of securing a more complete revenge. Such a powerful tribe as his need feel no misgiving in allowing a small party to enter their town; for, after that was done, they would be so completely at their mercy that there was no possibility of any explorer ever living to tell the tale.

He especially dwelt upon the undoubted influence possessed by Waggaman and Burkhardt. They would never consent to yield the influence they had held so long, nor could they be induced to share it with any of their own countrymen.

Grimcke and Ashman laughed at his fears, but strive as much as they chose, they could not help being affected more or less by his pessimistic views.

However, the brave fellow declared that he would accompany them on the hazardous journey, and stick by them to the end. If they could not survive, they would fall together.

By this time the night was far along. A careful scrutiny of the other bank failed to reveal anything of their enemies, though all believed there were plenty of them along the shore.

Ashman proposed, that now, since they were entirely

screened by the projecting shadow of the wood, they should cautiously push their way up the bank, as near as possible to the rapids, so as to lessen the distance that was to be passed on the morrow. There could be no objection to this, and adjusting themselves in the usual manner in the large canoe, they began the ascent of the river.

Naturally they would have kept close to the shore to escape, so far as they could, the force of the current, and the main object now was to prevent their movements being seen by the vigilant Aryks across the stream, who might resume hostilities before Ziffak could make his wishes known to them.

Our friends did not forget that a large body of these warriors had passed the Xingu above the rapids to reach the bank along which the craft was now stealing its way; but they had received such treatment that the survivors hurried from the vicinity.

Still there was a probability that after rallying from their repulse, more of them had swam across and were at that moment on the western shore, on the watch for just such a movement as was under way.

If this should prove the case, it could not be expected that Ziffak could interfere in time to prevent another sanguinary conflict; but that might come about, even if the explorers remained where they had stopped until daylight. If the Aryks were prepared to attack them while on the move, they could do so with equal effect while they were not in motion.

The increasing roar of the rapids was a great disadvantage, for it drowned all inferior noises and compelled our friends to depend on their eyesight alone to discover the approach of danger.

Edward S. Ellis

There was an involuntary shudder on the part of all, when they came opposite the scene of the desperate fight, and they hastened past without exchanging a word.

They had not much further to go when they found themselves, for the time, at the end of their voyage. It was impossible to ascend further, because of the rapids, which tossed the canoe about as though it were an eggshell.

A halt was therefore made, and, at the moment this took place, all observed that day was breaking, the light rapidly increasing in the direction of the Aryk village.

"*Just what I told you!*" exclaimed Jared Long, as the simultaneous discovery was made by all, that the forest around them was swarming with the vengeful savages, eager for another and bloodier joust at arms.

CHAPTER XVIII

THE NICK OF TIME

The peril which menaced the explorers was more frightful than any that they had been called upon to face since entering that mysterious land known by the name of the Matto Grosso.

The Aryks numbered more than half a hundred, all active, vigilant and armed with their fearful poisoned javelins. They had taken position among the trees on the western bank of the Xingu, at the base of the rapids, at the very point where the white men intended to shoulder their canoe and make their last portage.

Instead of being in the open, where they were in plain sight of the defenders, and fair targets for their unerring Winchesters, they were stationed behind the numerous trunks or lying on the ground, where little could be seen of them except their bushy heads and gleaming black eyes, as they glared with inextinguishable hate at the white men who had slain so many of their number.

The suspicious Long was looking in the direction, with the thought that if any ambush was attempted, that would be the very spot, when he caught sight of a dusky figure, as it

Edward S. Ellis

whisked from behind a narrow trunk to another that afforded better cover.

That hasty glance in the dim morning light revealed an alarming number of heads glaring around the trees and from among the undergrowth like so many wild beasts, aflame with fury and the exultation of savages who knew that their enemies were at last forced inextricably into their grasp.

So assured were the Aryks in fact that they showed a disposition to toy for a moment with their victims, as a cat does with a mouse before craunching it in her jaws. They brandished their weapons, danced grotesquely and uttered shrill shrieks audible above the deafening roar of the angry Xingu as it foamed through the rapids.

It was a fearful trap in which our friends found themselves, for it was impossible to advance or retreat, and it was madness to hope that they could again escape the shower of spears that were already poised in the air and ready to be launched.

Bippo and Pedros, with wild shrieks of terror bounded into the canoe, and wrapping the blankets around them, cowered in abject helpless dread of impending death. They were only an incumbrance, as they had proven in more than one crisis before.

But not one of the Caucasians showed the white feather. Disdaining to seek impossible shelter, they coolly prepared to die fighting, while exposed to the hurtling javelins, whose appalling effectiveness they knew too well.

But at this appalling juncture, when life hung on the passing moment, a piercing shout rang out above the roar of the waters.

It came from a point behind them, and, despite the imminent peril all three looked around.

A small canoe was darting across the Xingu toward them, so close to the foot of the rapids, that it danced about like a cork and seemed certain to be submerged every minute.

In this frail craft sat the giant Ziffak, propelling it across the furious swirl with such prodigious power that though the spume dashed over it, the boat was driven by the sheer power of his mighty arms under, above, and through the waters.

It was he who uttered the resounding cry which caused the wondering explorers to turn their heads, and stayed the uplifted arms of the venomous Aryks.

All saw the giant head chieftain of the Murhapas who repeated the shout and added an exclamation that was a command, forbidding his allies to hurl a single weapon.

They must have deemed him mad, but if so he was ten times more to be dreaded than if sane. Not a javelin was launched, but all stood motionless awaiting his arrival, and doubtless believing he meant them to pause only long enough to place himself at their head as the leader.

They must have thought, too, that his appearance so filled the whites with fear that their arms were paralyzed, for, though he was in direct range, not a hand of the foreigners was raised to do him hurt.

Coming with such tremendous speed, Ziffak occupied but a moment in passing the remaining distance. Before the prow of his boat could touch land, he flung the paddle aside, spurned the canoe with his foot, caught up his huge spear, and with one bound placed himself opposite the wondering trio of white men, while two more leaps landed him among the Aryks.

Grimcke, Ashman and Long had read aright the meaning of the amazing demonstration and calmly awaited the issue.

Pausing in the very middle of the dusky force, he addressed them in their native tongue, with savage gestures and a fierceness of tones which rendered every word audible amid the roaring tumult.

Only a second or two was required for him to finish his harangue, when he made a final command for them to fall back, emphasized by the swing of his tremendous arms.

No more striking proof could have been given of the sway of this mighty warrior over his vassals, than was shown by their instant obedience to the order, which fell upon them like the bursting of a thunderbolt from the clear summer sky.

They did not scatter and flee, for they had not been directed to do so, but skurried several rods back among the trees, so as to leave the way open for the explorers to pass around the rapids to the calmer waters above.

Ziffak did not remove his eyes from the natives, until he saw that his commands were not only obeyed, but that it was understood by them that the white men were not to be molested.

This extraordinary person had hastened to the other shore, in accordance with his pledge, only to learn from a couple of Aryks whom he met that the main body of warriors had again crossed the Xingu above the rapids, and were gathered in the wood waiting for the whites to walk into the trap set for them.

Had our friends remained where he left them, no danger would have been encountered, but, as we have shown, they moved up stream and came within a hair's-breadth of being wiped from the face of the earth before their powerful ally could interfere.

The breaking morning gave Ziffak his first knowledge of the mistake they had made, and, leaping into his canoe, he drove it across the stream with resistless speed, reaching the spot in the nick of time, and barely doing that, since he was forced to raise his voice while yet on the river, in order to hold the battle in suspense.

Having satisfied himself that everything was adjusted, Ziffak now turned around, and, without the least appearance of agitation on his swarthy countenance, signified that the path was open for them to continue their journey.

Reaching into the canoe, Ashman seized Bippo by the nape of the neck and hoisted him out on land. He did the same with Pedros, both of them howling in the extremity of mortal terror. Tearing the blankets from their bodies, he shouted for them to give their help in carrying the canoe and luggage around the rapids.

It was some minutes before they could comprehend in their blind way the situation. Finally, when they saw that their deaths were postponed, they lent their aid as eagerly as a couple of obedient dogs.

The sturdy whites were equally helpful, and the boat was quickly raised aloft and so adjusted that its well apportioned weight bore lightly upon the shoulders of all.

The sidelong glances which Bippo and Pedros cast at the Aryks as they moved up the bank, brought a smile to the whites who witnessed them. The poor fellows were ready to let go and drop down dead the moment they felt the puncture of the whizzing javelins.

The Professor was at the head of the strange procession bearing the boat on their shoulders. Like his companions, he moved with a springy, elastic step, for he had received the most striking proof possible of the friendship of Ziffak, and he foresaw the dazzling results that were to flow from such an alliance.

Had this remarkable savage been disposed to play them false, no better opportunity could have been given than that which occurred a few minutes before. All he had to do was to arrive on the spot a minute later: the Aryks would have left nothing for him except to view the dead bodies of the whites and their servants.

As for Jared Long, the doubter, he was willing to admit that he had made a grevious error of judgment. Had he thought that Ziffak suspected his misgivings, he would have taken the fellow's hand, and humbly begged his pardon.

CHAPTER XIX

THE JOURNEY'S END

The explorers, bearing the canoe with the luggage upon their shoulders, ascended at a steady gait the western bank of the Xingu. The cleared space which they had noticed on both sides of the river, caused by the furious overflow, continued, so that the progress was comparatively easy.

The din of the rapids was so loud that they could not have heard each other, except by shouting at the top of their voices, for which there was no call, since even Bippo and Pedros were now able to read the full meaning of the extraordinary incidents of the night.

Ashman looked around and ascertained that Ziffak was not bearing them company. None of the savages were in sight, though all would have been as eager as tigers to rend the white men to shreds had such permission been given.

The absence of the great leader caused no uneasiness on the part of any one of our friends. Strange indeed, would it have been had they felt any distrust of him after his late interference.

The sun appeared while the party were still pushing forward.

Edward S. Ellis

The sky was as clear as on the preceding day, and, though the temperature was quite warm, it was not unpleasantly so. Several causes contributed to the delightful coolness which renders the Matto Grosso one of the most attractive regions on the globe. The abundance of water, the endless stretch of forest, with few llanos of any extent, and, above all, the elevation of the plateau produce a moderation of temperature not met with in the lowlands, less than twenty degrees further south.

But the explorers were weary and in need of rest. It will be recalled that they found precious little opportunity for sleep during the preceding night, which marked the close of an unusually hard day's labor. They would have rested could they have done so, and now that the chance seemed to present itself, they wisely decided to wait a few hours before beginning the last stretch of water which lay between them and the villages of the Murhapas.

The halt was made at the top of the rapids, where the boat was carefully replaced in the river, the fracture made by Ziffak's javelin repaired, and everything adjusted for the resumption of their voyage. Then, with only the Professor on guard, the others lay down on their blankets and almost immediately sank into a deep, refreshing slumber.

Professor Grimcke, finding the care of the camp on his hands, took a careful survey of his surroundings, which were quite similar to those that had enclosed him many times before.

On both sides, stretched the almost endless Brazilian forest, within which a traveller might wander for weeks and months without coming upon any openings. In front was the Xingu, smooth, swift, and winding through the wilderness in such form that he could see only a short distance up stream.

Looking in the opposite direction, the agitation of the water was noticeable before breaking into rapids, similar, though in a less degree, to the rapids above Niagara Falls. The volume still preserved its remarkable purity and clearness, which enabled him to trace the shelving bottom a long way from where he stood.

Grimcke was somewhat of a philosopher, and always eager to make the best use of the time at his command. There was nothing more to be feared from the Aryks, and his situation, therefore, of guardian of his sleeping friends might be considered a sinecure.

His fishing line was soon arranged, and with some of the dried meat he had brought along serving for bait, he began piscatorial operations.

It will strike the reader as incredible, but in Borne portions of the Orinoco and other tropical rivers of South America, the fish are so abundant that they have been known to impede the progress of large vessels moving through the waters. While no such overflowing supply is found in the Xingu, yet they were so numerous that it required but a few minutes for the Professor to haul in more than enough to furnish the entire party with all they could eat at a single meal.

His next step was to start a fire, and prepare the coals for broiling. This was a simple task, and was completed before his friends finished their naps.

No pleasanter awakening could have come to them than that of opening their eyes and finding their breakfast awaiting their keen appetites. They fell to with a will, and, though saddened by the loss of two of their number, were filled with a strange delight at the prospect of their visit to the enchanted land.

Edward S. Ellis

The boat was launched, but there was not enough wind to make it worth while to spread the sail, which had often proven of such assistance, but the four pairs of arms swung the paddles with a vigor that sent the craft swiftly against the current. The Professor disposed of himself in the boat so that he slept while the others were at work.

Naturally the craft was kept as close to the bank as possible, so as to gain the benefit of the sluggish current. The trees having been swept from the margin of the Xingu, an open space was before the explorers throughout the entire distance.

Despite the glowing expectations of the party, there was enough in the prospect before them to cause serious thought. Long and Ashman consulted continually and saw that it would not do to felicitate themselves with the belief that all danger was at an end.

Two facts must be well weighed. Waggaman and Burkhardt were inimical to them. Whether they could be won over even to neutrality could not be determined until they were seen. For the present they must be classed as dangerous enemies.

Was it unreasonable to suspect that their influence with the terrible King Haffgo would prove superior to that of Ziffak? If so, what hope was there of the escape of the explorers after once intrusting themselves within the power of the tyrant?

But the immediate question which faced our friends was, whether it would do for them to reveal themselves to the Murhapas without again seeing their native friend. They deemed it probable that he had pushed on to the village, with the expectation of reaching it ahead of them and thus preparing the way for their reception.

This, however, was but a pretty theory which was as liable to be wrong as right. At any rate, Ziffak must reach his home ahead of or simultaneously with the whites. The latter continued using their paddles with steady vigor, until near noon, when they knew that considerably more than half the distance was passed.

They now began swaying their paddles less powerfully, for the feeling was strong upon them that they had approached as close as was prudent to the Murhapa village.

It was about this time, that they rounded a bend in the Xingu which gave them sight of the river for fully half a mile before another change in its course shut out all view. Naturally, they scanned the stream in quest of enemies, who were now likely to be quite close.

The first survey showed them a canoe coming down stream. It was near the middle and was approaching at a rapid rate.

Fred Ashman laid down his paddle and took up his binocular.

"It is Ziffak!" he exclaimed, passing the glass to Long.

"So it is and he is alone," was the reply of the astonished New Englander, who added an exclamation of surprise that he should be approaching from that direction. The only explanation was, that since last seeing him, he had made a journey to his home and was now returning to meet and convoy his friends to his own people.

Such proved to be the case, as he explained on joining them.

After the affair at the foot of the rapids, he paused long enough to make clear to the Aryks that not one of them was

Edward S. Ellis

to make another offensive movement against the whites under penalty of the most fearful punishment. He explained that these particular white men were the friends of all natives, and that they never would have harmed an Aryk had they not been forced to do so to save their own lives.

The cunning Ziffak dropped a hint that the newcomers were much better persons than the couple that had made their homes among the Murhapas for so many years. Then, having completed his business in that line, he struck through the forest at a high rate of speed and soon reached his own people.

He expected to find Waggaman and Burkhardt there, but they had not yet arrived. He explained to his brother the king what had taken place at the rapids of the Xingu and succeeded in gaining his promise of the king that he would allow the white men to enter the village without the sacrifice of their lives; but he was not willing that they should remain more than a couple of days. Indeed he gave such assent grudgingly and probably would have refused it altogether, but for the earnest pleading of his beloved Ariel, who insisted that it would be a partial recompense of the crime of three years previous.

This was the best that Ziffak, with all his influence at court could do, and indeed it was as much as he expected to accomplish. He admitted that Waggaman and Burkhardt were likely to interfere, but he did not believe they could do so to any serious extent, provided the white men themselves were circumspect in their behavior.

While this interesting interchange was going on, the two boats were side by side, so gently impelled that their progress was moderate and conversation pleasant. Thinking that the Professor had slept long enough, and that he ought to know the news, Fred Ashman turned to wake him; but to his surprise, the German met his look with a smile and the remark that he had heard every word spoken. Then he rose to a sitting posture, saluted Ziffak and proceeded to light his pipe.

The latter pleased the whites still further by explaining that he meant to keep them company for the rest of the distance. Despite his encouraging statements, they felt much easier with him as their escort.

By using their paddles with moderate vigor, they could reach their destination by the middle of the afternoon. There was no better hour to arrive, for the king was always in his best mood after enjoying his siesta, which was always completed by the time the sun was half-way down the sky.

It was to be expected also that before that hour, Waggaman and Burkhardt would spread the news of the expected coming of the wonderful strangers. They would do what they could, to excite distrust and enmity, but Ziffak was positive that since his brother had given his promise, it would be sacredly kept, and that for two days at least their stay at the village would be without peril to any one of the little company.

CHAPTER XX

AT THE MURHAPA VILLAGE

The sun was half-way down the sky when the canoe containing the explorers, and accompanied by the smaller craft impelled by Ziffak, rounded a bend of the upper Xingu and came in sight of the village of the Murhapas.

The herculean native gave an extra sweep of his paddle which sent his boat slightly in advance of the other, and, striking the shore, he sprang out and turned about to wait for them to disembark.

The scene was an impressive one, which every member of the company was sure to remember the rest of his life.

The huts in which these strange people made their homes were similar in structure to those of the Aryks, but instead of being built around the three sides of a rectangle, composed one row, numbering more than a hundred, and facing the river. They stood a hundred yards from the water, and being at the top of the sloping bank were above the reach of the most violent freshet that ever came down from the mountain-fed sources of the mighty Xingu.

The ground in front of this novel town was cleared of all

trees and undergrowth, but for most of the space was covered with bright green grass; the whole having the appearance of a well-kept lawn that had been artificially sodded or strewn with seed, which flourished with the luxuriance of every species of vegetation in that tropic country.

Not only in front, but on the sides and to the rear, for an extent of more than a hundred acres, the earth had been cleared with equal thoroughness and was growing abundant crops of cotton, tobacco, and edibles peculiar to the region.

The houses were separated by a space of several rods, so that the town itself extended a long way along the water. The dwellings, like those of the Aryks, consisted of a single story, with the door in the middle of the front, a window-like opening on each side of the same, roofed over with poles, covered with earth, leaves and grass, that were impervious to wind and storm.

It seemed to the astonished whites that the entire population had gathered along the shore to receive them. Several strange sights impressed them. The men were large, sinewy, bushy-haired and athletic. Some sported bows and arrows, but the majority by far carried the spears which the explorers held in such dread. There was no native, so far as they could see, who was the equal in size and strength of Ziffak, but they were so much the superiors of any natives encountered since leaving the Amazon, that it was easy to understand how they were the lords and masters of all the tribes with which they came in conflict.

We have spoken of the Murhapa houses as being but a single story in height. There was a single exception. In the middle of the town was a broader and larger structure than the others. It was two stories high and so much more marked in every respect that it was easy to decide that it was the residence or palace of Haffgo, the king of these people.

Another singular feature was noticed by our friends as they stepped from their canoe. Among the natives, who were mostly as dark of skin as Africans, was a sprinkling so different that the inference was that they belonged to some other race, or that nature was accustomed to play some strange freak in this almost unknown part of the world.

The king and his daughter Ariel had complexions as fair as the natives of Georgia and Persia, and yet Ziffak, a full brother of Haffgo, was as ebon-tinted as the darkest warrior of the tribe. Since the features of all were similar in a general way the cause was one that could not be explained.

It was a moment when the new-comers fully appreciated the value of a friend at court. They felt that had each possessed a dozen repeating Winchesters they would have been of no avail after leaving their canoe and entering the village. They had now placed their lives in the hands of Ziffak, and, should he choose to desert them, they were doomed; it was too late to retreat.

Many of the warriors scowled at the white men and their two helpers as though they would have been glad to impale them with their spears, but no demonstration was made. Evidently Ziffak possessed unlimited power and was backed by the pledge of the king.

Professor Grimcke was the first to step ashore, Ashman and Long following immediately. The three whites formed abreast, while Bippo and Pedros covered [Transcriber's note: cowered?] so close that it was hard for them to keep from stepping on their heels. Ziffak placed himself at the head, as the escort, and moved up the sloping bank with the dignity of a conqueror.

The women, showed more taste in their dress, for all wore loose-fitting gowns of native cloth, gaudily colored, though the children were attired similarly to the men, with little more than a breech cloth about the loins. Even the boys of a most tender age were each armed with a javelin, none of them, however, having the points of the weapons poisoned as did their fathers and elders when on the war-path.

Another striking characteristic of these people was the abundance of gold and diamond ornaments. Not a woman was visible from whose ears were not suspended heavy rings of the precious metal, while the majority had diamonds fastened in the gold, all of several carats' weight, and some so large and brilliant that they would have sold for immense sums in a civilized country.

The older females had not only rings hanging from their ears, but still more valuable ornaments depended from their noses. It would have enriched an army to loot the Murhapa village.

Each of the whites carried his Winchester, and Bippo and Pedros did not forget their almost harmless spears; but the rifle of Johnston was left behind with the valuable property.

At the moment of starting, Ziffak called to two warriors and said something in a commanding voice. They instantly hastened to the edge of the water and placed themselves in front of the large canoe. Their action left no doubt they were obeying an order to guard the treasures during the absence of the owners.

Reaching the top of the bank, the party were in what might be called the main or only street of the town. The grass had been worn smooth by the feet of the villagers, among whom

Edward S. Ellis

was not a dog, cat, horse, and, indeed, any four-footed animal.

The visitors had landed near the lower end of the village, so that it was necessary to walk some way before reaching the house of the king, which was their destination.

As they started, the whole population began falling in behind them. The terrified Bippo and Pedros shrank still closer to those in front, trembling and affrighted, for the experience to which they were subjected was enough to upset them morally, mentally and physically.

Ziffak turned his head with such a threatening scowl that the foremost instantly fell back, dreading his vengeance, but when he faced the other way, they began crowding forward again.

There must have been that in the appearance and action of Bippo and Pedros which excited the latent mirth of the Murhapas, for say what we may, the trait exists in a greater or less degree in all human beings. One of them reached forward with his javelin and gave Bippo a sharp prick. With a howl, he leaped several feet in air and yelled that he was killed.

There was an instant expansion of dark faces into grins, showing an endless array of black stained, teeth, for the spear point was not poisoned, and the incident caused a laugh on the part of his white friends when they came to know the whole truth.

But the author of the practical joke had reckoned without his host. The cry had hardly escaped the victim, when Ziffak bounded to the rear like a cyclone. The fellow who was a full grown warrior was still grinning with delight, when he found himself in the terrific grasp of the head chieftain. It was then his turn to utter a shriek of affright, which availed him nothing.

Ziffak first smote him to the earth by a single tremendous blow. Then, before he could rise to his feet, he grasped his ankles, one with either hand, and swung him round his head, as a child whirls a sling, before throwing the stone.

To the awed spectators he seemed a black ring of fire, so dizzyingly swift were the gyrations, from the midst of which came a buzzing moan of terror.

Only for a second or two was he subjected to this torture. Suddenly Ziffak ran toward the Xingu and then let go of the ankles. The black, limp object went spinning far out in the air, as if driven from some enormous catapult.

Across the remaining space he went, falling several feet from shore and disappearing beneath the surface. But such fellows are extinguished with difficulty, and the cold water quickly revived him.

By and by he came up, blew the moisture from his mouth, swam to shore, climbed timidly out, and, sneaking up the bank again, humbly took his place at the rear of the procession.

But Ziffak, having disposed of the joker, paid no further attention to him, caring naught whether he swam or was drowned. The lesson was one that he would not forget, and produced a salutary effect upon the rest of the multitude. They instantly fell back so far that Bippo, finding he had not been seriously hurt, saw that he was safe from further disturbance.

Edward S. Ellis

It was only a few minutes later that Ziffak halted, his friends immediately doing the same.

The cause was apparent: they had reached the dwelling place of Haffgo king of the Murhapas.

CHAPTER XXI

HAFFGO, KING OF THE MURHAPAS

It was a memorable interview which the explorers held with Haffgo, king of the mighty Murhapas.

Since Bippo and Pedros were servants, they were not admitted to an audience with the potentate. Ziffak conducted the others into the hut adjoining the palace. This was his own building, where his aged mother had charge. She understood matters from her son, and the frightened fellows were made to feel that they were safe for a time from the annoyances and persecutions of the multitude.

The apartment was an oblong one, being at the front, and was characteristically furnished. Instead of the smooth bare ground which formed the floors of the other buildings, the palace was entirely covered with the skins of wild animals, gaudily stained. The whole looked like a gorgeous, oriental carpet, which was as soft as down to the tread.

There were no chairs or benches for auditors, for no one presumed to sit in the presence of majesty. The walls were hung with the same species of ornamented furs, set off here and there by spears, bows and arrows, arranged in fantastic fashion.

At the further end of the apartment, was a platform several feet high, with a broad seat, covered with still more brilliant peltries, a footstool, and on each side a vase of magnificent flowers. These vases were of native manufacture, beautifully ornamented, while the flowers were of a radiant loveliness, such as are seen nowhere outside of tropical countries. Their delicious fragrance filled the apartment and affected the strangers the moment the blanket was pulled aside by Ziffak and they stepped within the royal reception room.

On each side was a broad open window, without glass, which admitted enough sunlight to flood the place with illumination.

At the right of the dais or throne, the curtains were draped so as to serve as a door for the king or any member of the royal household to enter or withdraw.

On this barbaric throne sat the extraordinary personage known as King Haffgo, ruler of the warlike Murhapas.

To say the least, his appearance was stunning, if not bewildering.

In the first place, it maybe doubted whether the intrinsic value of his crown was not the equal of any that can be found to-day in the monarchical countries of Europe, Asia or Africa. Its foundation seemed to be a network of golden wire, in which were set scores upon scores of diamonds, weighing from five to ten carats apiece, with a central sun the equal of the great Pitt diamond. The coruscations from these brilliants were overwhelming. As the king moved his head while speaking, every hue of the rainbow flashed and scintillated, the rays at times seeming to dart entirely across the room.

In addition, the neck of Haffgo was encircled by a double string of the same dazzling jewels, of hardly less magnitude; while the wrist of the right hand, which rested on a large javelin, was clasped by a golden bracelet of what appeared to be living fire.

The king was dressed in a species of thin cloth, gathered by a girdle at the waist. The crimson tint of this garment was relieved by figures of the sun, moon and stars, of dragons, birds, beasts and reptiles in gold. One of his feet was visible, disclosing a species of sandal such as is seen among the natives of the East Indies.

Had King Haffgo been encountered anywhere else, he would have been set down as a European with an unusually fair complexion. It bore no liking to that of the African or native Murhapa. His skin had none of that chalky, transparent appearance shown by the Albinos, but was almost pinkish and ruddy.

His bushy hair was not white, but of a decided brown, his eyes hazel, his nose Roman, with a strong chin and a keen expression, such as was natural to a man who had reigned an absolute autocrat all his life.

He was about fifty years of age, but his face was wrinkled like a man of threescore and more.

King Haffgo was seated on his throne when his visitors were ushered into his presence, as though he expected and was waiting for them.

The white men were unacquainted with the etiquette prevailing in this barbaric court, but there are certain cere-monies which are received as expressive of courtesy and obeisance the world over.

Ziffak gave no instructions; but, placing himself at the side of Professor Grimcke on the left, he surveyed his friends with much curiosity, as if waiting to see how they would conduct themselves.

Grimcke, Long and Ashman removed their hats and bowed slowly, bending their heads almost to their knees. Then, as they straightened up again, the Professor, who took upon himself the duty of spokesman, said:

"We greet the great King Haffgo, and beg that he will accept the homage of his brothers from their homes near the great water."

"Why do my brothers come from their homes to hunt out the king of the Murhapas, when he has not asked them to come?"

These words were uttered almost exactly as given. The accent was thick and somewhat broken, but they showed an astonishing command of the English tongue, and proved that Waggaman and Burkhardt had found some exceedingly apt pupils among this people.

It is not necessary to give the interview in detail. There was a certain stateliness about the manner of the king which was remarkably becoming. His guests had prepared themselves, when starting out on their exploring enterprise, to make friends, by providing a large supply of gaudy trinkets, such as is always pleasing to the average savage; but, when they saw the wonderful crown and diamond ornaments of this autocrat, they were ashamed to let the baubles in their possession be seen.

They consisted mainly of children's toys; and, since they were entirely different from anything in the country,

Professor Grimcke finally made bold to offer them, with another low obeisance, to his majesty. The latter may have been delighted, but, if so, he did not allow it to appear in his face or manner.

Fred Ashman handed him two brightly-polished knives, fashioned somewhat after the familiar Bowie pattern, and, despite his reserve, it was easy to see that they pleased him more than anything else.

Jared Long's present was a handsomely-carved meerschaum pipe. The king was an inveterate smoker, and, even if he didn't do anything more than nod his head when it was placed in his hand, he ought to have been very grateful.

Despite the pains which our friends took to win the good will of King Haffgo, it was apparent to all three that their visit was not welcome. Waggaman and Burkhardt may not have whispered anything in his ear about them, but the ruler was thoroughly filled with a distrust of all white men, the only exceptions being the ones that were the cause of this distrust.

Being a man of unquestioned native sagacity, it needed nothing more from his first guests than their accounts of what the other race was doing in the cities and towns along the sea coasts. Any people who builded canoes large enough to cross the awful waste of waters in quest of diamonds and gold, were sure to seize the chance to force their way up the Xingu where much more boundless wealth awaited them.

The famous diamond mines of Brazil were not very far from this portion of the Matto Grosso, and the pains which the emperors of Brazil had taken to draw a part of their riches from the earth was all the proof Haffgo could ask of the rapacity of the nations which called themselves civilized.

Edward S. Ellis

Now, while this remarkable ruler could not always make certain that no white men should enter his dominions, there remained a very good chance of preventing such intruders from getting away again, carrying the glowing accounts of what they had discovered. So long as he could maintain this condition of affairs, so long was he safe; for if he "absorbed" every foreigner ascending the Xingu, the supply could never exceed the demand.

The King conversed with not only the Professor, but with Long and Ashman in turn. They were as deferential as they knew how to be, but all the same, their sagacity told them he bore them no good will, and would have been much better pleased had the Aryks wiped them out before they ascended the rapids.

At the conclusion of the interview, which lasted about half an hour, the King Haffgo informed them they were at liberty to remain two days in the village, during which they were not to pass outside its boundaries. At the expiration of the period named, they would be allowed to descend the Xingu to their homes, under their pledge to tell no person what they had seen and learned about the Murhapas.

CHAPTER XXII

ARIEL THE BEAUTIFUL

It will be understood that during the interview described, the three white men stood near the front entrance to the royal apartment with their faces turned toward King Haffgo.

In this position each made good use of his eyes and Fred Ashman's, from some cause or other, continually wandered to the draped curtains at the right of the ruler, between which he must pass when entering or leaving that part of his residence.

It was while his gaze was used on these curtains that he saw them gently agitated in a way which left no doubt that some person on the other side was the cause.

By and by he discerned part of a dainty hand, and the next minute became aware that a pair of the most beautifully lustrous eyes on which he had ever gazed was peering into the apartment.

"*It is Ariel*," was his instant thought, "and she as listening to the words that we are speaking."

The thought had hardly found shape, when one eye, a part of

a lovely face and the top of the head were discerned, as the owner, giving rein to her curiosity, ventured upon a little further view of the visitors.

Then, as if conscious of her breach of etiquette, she withdrew, like a flash, from view altogether.

But he knew it was only for a brief interval, and sure enough, the eyes speedily appeared at another portion of the curtains, where the beauteous princess must have believed she was not observed, for she looked steadily at the faces of the visitors, with a depth of interest that it was vain for her to attempt to conceal.

The heart of Fred Ashman gave a flutter, when he realized that the midnight orbs were fastened upon *him*, and, evidently studying his countenance with more interest than those of his companions.

Feeling a peculiar boldness, because of the strange situation in which he was placed, he deliberately smiled at the unknown one.

She could not have vanished more suddenly had she been snatched away by the hand of some ogre.

A pang shot through Fred's heart, as he felt that he had driven away the enchantress by his own forwardness. He reproached himself bitterly for having overreached himself.

But while he was lamenting, he once more discovered the eyes, rivalling the diamonds in the crown of her royal father, slyly viewing him from the other side of the curtain. This time the fair one took care that no part of her countenance was visible, and the young man was equally guarded for the time, not to betray his sweet knowledge of the other's scrutiny.

It was at this juncture, that King Haffgo addressed some pointed questions to Ashman who was forced to withdraw his gaze from the marvellously attractive sight, and fasten it upon the rugged and wrinkled countenance of the king of the Murhapas.

But those eyes were in his field of vision, and, even while speaking to the potentate, his glance continually wandered to the orbs which attracted him as the lodestone draws the magnet.

But alas! the American forgot a fact of the first importance: the eyes of the father were as observant as those of his only child. He saw the furtive glances at the curtains, and a slight rustling at his right hand told him that his beloved Ariel, with the curiosity of her sex, was playing the eavesdropper.

The indulgent father would have cared nothing for this, had he not discovered the extraordinary interest which one of his three callers manifested in his child. In that moment, the distrust which he felt of the strange race was turned to violent hatred toward one of its members, because of his unpardonable insolence in daring to return the gaze with a smile.

The king suddenly leaned the javelin in his hand against the chair in which he was sitting, and partly rose from his seat as if about to descend from the throne. Instead of doing so, he leaned slightly to one side, and, with a quick movement, seized one of the curtains and snatched it aside.

The act, which was like the flitting of a bird's wing, caused Ariel, his daughter, to stand forth fully revealed!

Edward S. Ellis

If the white men had been dazzled by the amazing collection of diamonds on the brow of the king, it may be said that they were now blinded for the moment by the vision of loveliness which burst upon them, like the unexpected emergence of the sun from behind a dark cloud.

Before the princess could rally from her bewilderment, her father sharply commanded her to advance. She knew that that affectionate parent could be stern and cruel as well as loving and affectionate, and with her eyes bent modestly on the floor she stepped forward and stood beside him.

Her hair, instead of being auburn like her parent's, was as black as the raven's wing. It hung in luxuriant wavy masses below her waist, being gathered by a white clasp of burnished silver at the back of the neck, without which it would have enveloped all the upper part of her body in its fleecy veil.

Her gown of spotless white, composed of native cloth, as fine as satin, was without any ornament. It was encircled at the waist by a golden girdle, falling in folds which concealed the rest of the figure, leaving only one Cinderella-like foot to twinkle from the front, like a jewel of rare beauty.

But no eye could fail to see that the slight girlish figure was of ravishing perfection. The waist was slender, the partly revealed arms were as delicate as lilies, the tiny hands with their tapering fingers were like those of a fairy, while the countenance was one of the fairest that ever sun shone on.

The contour was such as Rubens delighted to place on canvas, and that Michael Angelo loved to carve from the snowy marble. The Grecian nose, the small mouth, the white teeth, unstained like those of her countrymen and country-women, the wealth of hair, the lustrous, soulful eyes, the sea-shell-like tint of the cheeks, all these fell upon the startled vision of the explorers with such overpowering suddenness that for the moment they believed they were dreaming, or that some trick of magic revealed to them a picture which had no reality.

"Look upon the white men!" commanded the king speaking in English, and with a sternness which left disobedience out of the question; "look, I say, for never will come the opportunity to see them again."

It was then that Ariel raised her eyes, and turned them toward the trio, gazing at no one in particular—for she knew her parent was closely studying her—but seeming to fix them upon some one miles behind them.

Grimcke, Long and Ashman again bowed their heads almost to the ground, and, feeling that the interview was over, began withdrawing.

Like the vassals leaving the presence of their sovereign, they did so walking backward, with their faces toward the throne, and making a low obeisance with each step.

The king looked steadily at them, without inclining his head or making the slightest acknowledgment of the salutation. Had not Fred Ashman been mad with the intoxication of his new, overwhelming passion, he would have observed that which was noticed by Grimcke and Long: the King was watching him.

The young American hardly raised his gaze from the floor, until in his retreat, he found himself at the entrance, by which all three had come in to the apartment. His companions had made their final obeisance and disappeared, while he was left with Ziffak standing near the middle of the apartment, his pose such that he could glance at his royal relative or at him without shifting his body.

It now became Fred's duty to assume the perpendicular, in order to effect a graceful withdrawal.

As he came upright once more, he looked straight into the countenance of the scowling king. Then—he could not help it—his eyes flashed in the face of the blushing Ariel, who was gazing fixedly at him, and he smiled and saluted her.

It was a daring thing to do, with the eyes of the king and the head chieftain upon him. He never understood how it was that it was done. The salutation might have been forgiven, but that smile was an offense like smiting King Haffgo's countenance with the back of the open hand.

But wonder of wonders! the ruby lips of the radiant beauty parted for an instant in the faintest possible smile which lit up her countenance like a burst of sunshine. Ashman noticed not the diamond bracelet and necklace, which flashed in all their prismatic beauty, but knew only that she had returned the smile of recognition. For that boon he would have risked life a thousand times over.

Both Ziffak and the king were looking at the white man at the moment; but, as if suspicion had entered the brain of the infuriated monarch, he quickly shifted his head and glared at his daughter.

The movement was like the dart of a serpent, but that shadowy smile on the face of Ariel had passed, as the lightning flash cleaves the midnight, leaving the darkness deeper than before.

The king saw it not, and well for his child that so it was; for, much as he cherished her, he would have smitten her to the earth had he dreamed that she ventured on such a response to the impudence of the white man, whose very life was his own only through the sufferance of King Haffgo.

Not until Fred Ashman found himself in the air on the outside of the place did he realize what he had done. He feared that he had committed a fatal indiscretion, but when he asked, himself whether he would recall it if he could, his heart said "No."

The afternoon was drawing to a close, and there was a sensible coolness in the air. The natives who had remained standing round the front of the palace, when the explorers first went inside, had grown tired of waiting and, scattered in different directions. The Murhapa village wore its usual appearance, so in contrast with what met the eyes of our friends when they first saw it.

The Professor and the New Englander were waiting near the door for Ashman to join them. As he came out, the former shook his head, with a laugh, as an intimation that the young man in the ardor of his interest had made a mistake.

Fred admitted that possibly he had forgotten himself, but added that it was now too late to recall what had been done, and he was not sure that he would do so, if the opportunity were given.

"At any rate," said he, "we are promised safe treatment for a couple of days, provided we don't stray off or misbehave ourselves. Our visit can't amount to anything after all, since we must start for home whenever King Haffgo gives his command."

"A good deal may take place in two days," said the Professor significantly.

"And a good deal *after* five days," was the more significant remark of Jared Long.

It was evident from these declarations that Grimcke and Long had in mind the same thought; which came to Ashman himself, when the ruler of the Murhapas made known to his guests that they must take their departure within such a brief period.

While no one of the three would have dared to signify dissent, yet they were not the men to come so many hundred miles, forcing their way through endless dangers to turn about and retrace their steps at the command of a savage who looked upon himself as king, simply because he was able to lord it over a horde of barbarians.

It was no place to discuss their plans, in front of the "palace," especially as the natives were beginning to gather around them again, and among them it was certain was more than one who understood the English tongue "as she is spoke."

They were waiting for the coming of Ziffak, who was still within. He was their chaperon, and without his guidance, they did not dare to move from the spot.

"Hark!" suddenly exclaimed the Professor, raising his hand as a signal for the whispering to cease.

The sound of voices was heard inside. They recognized the tones of Ziffak, to which they had become accustomed since the previous night. Those of King Haffgo were also distinguishable, and there could be no doubt to whom the low silvery accents heard only occasionally belonged.

The alarming feature of it all was, that the king was in an unmistakably angry mood. He not only talked fast but he talked loud, sure evidence of his excited feelings. It sounded as if Ziffak was striving to placate him, but his royal brother grew more savage each moment.

The words of all were uttered in the Murhapa tongue, so that the listeners could form no idea of their meaning. Had they been able to do so, it is safe to say that they would have been in anything but a comfortable frame of mind.

Edward S. Ellis

CHAPTER XXIII

THE SHADOW OF DANGER

A few minutes later, Ziffak came through the door of the king's residence and greeted the explorers.

His dusky countenance showed unmistakable traces of emotion, but like a true warrior, he knew how to govern his feelings. When he spoke, there was no agitation perceptible in his voice.

He motioned to his friends to enter the adjoining hut, where Bippo and Pedros had been left. The Professor showing a natural timidity, he stepped forward and led the way.

Immediately, the party found themselves within a structure, which while no larger than the others, still, in view of the royal prerogatives of the occupant perhaps, possessed more conveniences. The lower apartment, or rather floor, was separated into three divisions, the front being that in which the cooking was done, while serving also for a sitting and general reception room.

The mother of Ziffak and King Haffgo was a tall, muscular widow of threescore and ten, much wrinkled, but strong and active on her feet. Her countenance was darker if possible than that of the head chieftain, making it the more wonderful that Haffgo should be the reverse in that respect of both.

The royal mother paid little heed to her visitors, probably believing they were able to take care of themselves without help from her. Indeed, shortly after the white men entered, she took her departure, and was not seen again until dark, when she came in to help provide them with their evening meal.

Bippo and Pedros finding themselves safe at last were doing what they could to make up for the sleepless nights and hard labor they had undergone on their way thither. They were stretched upon some skins in one corner, sleeping heavily and refreshingly.

Ziffak sat on the floor with the whites. It was apparent from his manner that he was on the point of making a communication of importance, but he seemed to change his mind suddenly, and, for a time, spoke upon matters of such trivial account that his listeners were surprised.

The next astonishing thing which he did was to declare that the stories he gave to Ashman the night before, when made a prisoner by him were fables. There was no enchanted lake in the neighborhood, and his account of the burning mountain was a myth, as were his yarns about the diamonds obtained from the same mountain.

The Professor nodded his head, laughed and said he was glad to be told that; for, while he wished to believe their good friend, when he was in earnest, he found it hard to swallow those marvellous narratives which exceeded anything that had ever come to their ears.

Long and Ashman also expressed great relief at the naive

Edward S. Ellis

confession of the head chieftain. All the same, however, not one of them was deceived by the fellow's subterfuge.

They knew that the stories which Ziffak related on the shore of the Xingu were true. Seized at that time by a burst of confidence, he had unburdened himself to the young man for whom he formed such deep admiration.

Since that time, and especially since his angry interview with his royal brother, he appreciated the grievous mistake he made and was now anxious to recall it. He, therefore, declared the accounts to be of the Munchausen order. His listeners read his purpose and it suited them to let him think they accepted every word of his remarkable recantation.

He impressed upon them that the king was angry because of their coming to his village. Indeed Ziffak was afraid that he would recall his permission to allow them to stay the two days, and might compel them to leave that night.

This was startling news, and, when Ziffak was pressed, he admitted that during his absence on the Xingu to meet them, Waggaman and Burkhardt had returned and secured an audience with His Majesty. This explained the new phase of matters and was anything but welcome information, but there was no help for it.

The Professor asked Ziffak whether he could not bring the two white men to his home, in order that an interview might be had. If that could be done, Grimcke was hopeful that a better understanding could be established, but the head chieftain replied that he had not seen either of the white men since he returned, nor did he know where to find them. They occupied a building on the opposite side of the king's home, but he was told they were not there. No doubt they were purposely keeping out of the way of the new-comers.

Suddenly Ashman asked their friend whether there was any objection to his taking a stroll around the village and whether he was likely to be molested. Ziffak promptly replied that there could be no earthly objection to anything of that nature, and springing to his feet, gun in hand, he bade his friends good-bye, saying he expected to be back with them at the end of an hour or so.

It cannot be said that Ashman had any special errand in view, when he formed this resolution, which was explainable upon the well known laws governing the human mind.

He was tired of idleness. The prospect of sitting for hours in the darkening apartment, talking with Ziffak, who, instead of being willing to give information, was doing his most to withhold it, was not inviting, but beyond this, he was restless because he was haunted by those marvellous eyes, peeping from behind the curtain in the king's room, and that smile of recognition when the gaze of the two met, thrilled him with a new and strange emotion.

It was this feeling which drove him forth. He wanted to escape the prying scrutiny of his friends, who, he fancied, suspected his secret. He wanted to walk in the open air and think and revel in the bliss of his new delight.

It was growing dark, when he stepped outside of the building. There was no light visible in any direction, though there would be plenty of it later on. The natives appeared to be moving aimlessly about, and one or two near at hand scrutinized him curiously, but they neither spoke nor made any movement to annoy him. They had not yet forgotten the lesson given by Ziffak some hours before.

To escape attention, he walked toward the river, passing down the long sloping bank, until he reached the open,

Edward S. Ellis

cleared space which has been referred to as caused by the overflow of the water. Here the walking was easy, and, turning his face up stream, he walked slowly as a man does who is in deep thought.

A man who is revelling in the first dream of love is not the one to pay close attention to his surroundings. He is so apt to be rapt in his own sweet meditations, that he fails in the most ordinary observation.

Reaching the bottom of the slope, Ashman glanced behind and on his right. He caught glimpses of several figures moving about like shadows, but so far as he could judge, none of them was interested in him. Dismissing them from his mind, he moved on.

He had walked less than one-third of the length of the village front, when the form of a man slipped softly down the incline, following in his footsteps and moving as silently as a Murhapa warrior tracking his foe through the forest.

He was dressed similarly to the American, having the same style of Panama hat, shirt and boots, and he carried a rifle in his hand. Being of the same race, he ought to have been a friend, but when the bright moonlight fell upon his face, it showed the countenance of a demon.

He was Burkhardt, an escaped convict, who had lived for five years among the Murhapas, and he was seeking the life of Fred Ashman, who, in his enchanting visions of love, never dreamed of the awful shadow stealing upon him.

CHAPTER XXIV

YOUNG LOVE'S DREAM

What in all the world so sweet as young love's dream? It is the old, old story, and yet it is as new and fresh and blissful to the soul as it will be to the end of time, or until these natures of ours are changed by the same Hand that framed them.

What more bewitching romance could cast its halo about the divine passion than that which enshrined the affection of Fred Ashman for the wonderful Ariel, the only child of the grim Haffgo, king of the Murhapas?

He had met and chatted and exchanged glances with the beauties of his own clime, and yet his heart remained unscathed. He reverenced the sex to which his adored mother and sister belonged, and yet never had he felt the thrill that stirred his nature to the profoundest depths, when his eyes met those of the barbarian princess and the two smiled without either uttering a word.

"What care I for the gold and the diamonds and the precious stones of the Matto Grosso?" the ardent lover asked himself; "is not she the Koh-i-noor of them all?—the one gem whose preciousness is worth more than all the world?"

He was willing that the Professor and Jared Long should risk their lives in searching for the enchanted lake, and the burning mountain where such priceless wealth existed. Thousands of their kind had done it before, and countless thousands would follow in their footsteps through the generations to come.

But as for *him*, a new mission had broken upon his consciousness; he had a sacred duty to perform. Somewhere, in this broad world, a human soul is always waiting for its mate. Perchance it never comes, and the weary one may be joined to that which heaven never intended it to be joined, or it repines and goes to the grave unloved.

Fred Ashman was as sure as if he heard a voice from the stars, telling him that Ariel, the daughter of Haffgo, was his other self. He could never rest, he could not really live until it should be his lot to carry her from this lonely wilderness to his own home thousands of miles away.

To the young lover, aglow and happy in his new passion, all things are possible. It is he who can appreciate even the days of chivalry, when the valiant knight went forth, with lance and buckler to win his lady against all comers, counting it his highest happiness to face the perils of flood and field if perchance he could but win her smile.

And yet, amid all the roseate dreams which fairly lifted Fred Ashman from the gross earth, he could not entirely lose sight of his peculiar situation and the formidable difficulties which environed his path. He would not admit they were insurmountable, but they were hard to climb.

To come down to facts, he felt that the first, and, indeed, the indispensable step was to secure a meeting with the princess that had taken such complete possession of his heart.

Guarded as she was by her father, who was sure to resent with instant death any such presumption on his part, he might well shrink from the appalling attempt; but love has many ways of picking the locks that may be fastened to keep hearts apart.

"Ziffak!"

That was the name which came to his tongue again and again, with the question whether his friendship could not be enlisted on the side of the youth, who had come so strangely to the Murhapa village. He was a shrewd fellow who must suspect the truth of those stolen glances. He had shown a sudden and strong affection for the explorers, and especially for Ashman to whom he surrendered. Was what friendship strong enough to lead him to a step that would insure a rupture with his royal brother and probably bring about war in his little kingdom?

"I wonder what revelation he was on the point of making when he sat down with us in his mother's home," Ashman muttered, as he slowly walked along the bank of the Upper Xingu, unmindful of the creeping shadow behind him.

That it bore upon that interview and related to the angry quarrel he did not doubt, but he could only conjecture its nature which was not encouraging when he recalled that Ziffak had told him and his friends, without protest on his part, that they were likely to be compelled to leave the village that night.

Ashman ceased in his walk, for he saw, in spite of his absorbing reverie, that he had passed above the uppermost house of the village. The condition under which he was allowed to stay in peace, even for a brief time, was that he should not wander beyond the limits of the town.

It was useless to excite resentment without reason, and he was about to turn and retrace his steps, when a slight rustling of the undergrowth, which marked the boundary of the forest on the south caused him to turn his head, stop, and hold his rifle ready for danger.

His old habit of caution came back the instant peril seemed to threaten.

While he debated whether to advance and force the stranger to reveal himself, the outlines of a form were distinguished and a slight figure stepped forth in the moonlight.

Ashman's heart seemed to stop beating and life itself hang in suspense, when he recognized the very being that had taken such full possession of his thoughts.

Ay, Ariel, daughter of King Haffgo, stood before him.

For a moment, neither spoke or moved. It was not strange perhaps that she was the first to recover the power of utterance.

Advancing timidly, she said in a tremulous voice and with an accent just broken enough to make it all the sweeter:

"You are in danger and I could not help coming to tell you."

"Heaven bless you!" he exclaimed, taking a step toward her, but still observing a respectful distance. "You have braved danger yourself to give me the warning."

"I left my home and waited for a chance to speak to you; I dared not go to the door of Ziffak's house for I would have been seen. Then, while I was wondering what to do, I saw you come forth and walk toward the river. I thought you would go to the end of the village, so I hurried on and hid among the bushes until I could speak to you without any one seeing me."

Ashman's head was in a swirl. He was trembling in every limb, while she seemed to be devoid of any agitation whatever.

"Your father King Haffgo was angry this afternoon, because I looked at you; but," added the lover, "I could not have helped doing it, if I knew my life would have paid for the act. Ziffak told me about you, so you see I did not feel that you were a stranger, even though I then saw you for the first time and never heard the music of your voice until now."

"The king is angry," said she, withdrawing a little as the happy fellow took another step; "he says you shall be killed, but Ziffak persuaded him to say your life should be spared if you went away to-night."

Ashman felt another delicious thrill as he reflected that if such were the understanding, there would seem to be no cause for the lovely Ariel to come thus far out of her way to repeat what Ziffak was sure to explain before the departure of the explorers.

Ah, it must have been because of her interest in him that she had sought this perilous stolen interview.

"Well, then," said he mournfully, "I must depart and never see you again. Death would be preferable to *that*!"

"But you may come back some time," said she in such a tremulous, hesitating voice, that he impulsively sprang forward and caught her dainty hand before she could escape him.

"O don't!" she plead like a timid bird, striving to withdraw the imprisoned fingers which he still held fast.

"Nay, but you must, if I am never to see you again," he exclaimed vehemently; "O, Ariel, I had hoped that I might stay here until I could see and talk with you and tell you that I can never, never leave you; that if I go, you must go with me; I will take you to my home which is many many long miles away, but I will be your slave; I will love you; I will make you happy; you shall never sigh for the land and the people you leave behind you—"

There is no saying when the impetuous lover would have stopped his wooing in this cyclone-like fashion hut for an alarming interruption. He had been smitten profoundly, and the urgency of the case impelled him to an ardor which could not have found expression under any other conditions; but, all the time the frightened maiden was striving to free her imprisoned hand, and the lover felt he ought to release it but could not.

Suddenly she ceased her efforts and looked beyond him with a gasp and such a startled expression, that he knew some unusual cause had produced it.

CHAPTER XXV

ZIFFAK'S BLOW

Ziffak, head chieftain of the Murhapas, was a shrewder and more far-seeing man than even his white friends suspected.

He had been the first to observe the significant glances of Fred Ashman at the hanging curtains, as he was the first to detect the presence of his beloved niece behind them.

Although King Haffgo saw not the smile which flitted over the face of his daughter, when her eyes met those of the young American, yet Ziffak observed it, and he could not have translated it wrongly had he wished to do so.

An intimation has been given of the nature of the quarrel between Ziffak and his royal brother. The latter was so infuriated that he declared that every one of the white men should die. Ziffak reminded him of his pledge that they should be safe for two days, a pledge that he had repeated in their presence.

But in his hot anger, Ziffak said, he would break that pledge. One of the explorers had dared to look upon the face of Ariel and smile. Had he detected her returning it, he would have driven his javelin through her body as she stood beside him.

Ziffak gave no hint of what he had observed.

The head chieftain was not afraid to brave his brother to his face; but he wisely forbore carrying the quarrel beyond the point of reconciliation. He told his brother that he was so beside himself that he forgot he was a Murhapa who never broke his word. But if the king insisted, he would see that the white men took their departure before the rising of the morrow's sun.

King Haffgo consented that if that was done, he would permit them to go in peace. It was Ziffak's hope that his brother, after his anger had time to cool, would modify his last declaration still further and allow them to stay their two days, that led him to qualify his remark about the necessity of their withdrawing that night.

The same cunning which stood the head chieftain so well during this stormy interview remained with him to the end. While he and his brother were wrangling, Ariel stood mute and with bowed head. She durst not speak, but withdrew only a minute or two before her parent.

Ziffak was still warmly attached to Ashman, and was willing to risk his life in his behalf. Knowing that Waggaman and Burkhardt had had much to do with stirring the resentment of the king, he was angry enough to slay both of them.

When the most peculiar situation is considered, however, it is hardly safe to believe the head chieftain was ready to go to the length of helping to bring about a meeting between the lovers.

He understood his niece well enough to know that despite the fury of her parent, she would brave a good deal to exchange words with the handsome stranger that had made such an impression on his heart.

So long as this young man remained in Ziffak's house, so long was it impossible for such meeting to take place; but, when Ashman sprang up and announced his intention of taking a stroll, Ziffak believed that it was with the intention of trying to see Ariel. That is to say, he suspected what really came to pass, though it was not in the mind of the youth.

Ashman had not been gone long, when Ziffak made an excuse to withdraw, saying he meant to find out, if he could, where Waggaman and Burkhardt were hiding. He counselled the Professor and the New Englander to stay where they were until his return, which he promised should not be long deferred.

Neither Grimcke nor Long dreamt of the object of their dusky friend in leaving, and as the mother of the Murhapa reappeared about that time and started a fire, with a view of preparing their evening meal, they concluded that the best thing for them was to follow the advice of the brave fellow.

The instant Ziffak was on the outside of his own house, he became as alert as a cat scenting a mouse. He held his ponderous javelin with its poisoned tip in his right hand, and he looked keenly about in the gathering gloom.

A warrior stopped in front of him and made a respectful inquiry about the white men. Ziffak uttered such an angry reply and raised his weapon so menacingly that the native skurried away in terror of his life.

All at once the keen black eyes caught sight of a small, petite figure as it vanished in the darkness. He smiled, for he recognized Ariel on her way to the upper end of the village. He knew on the instant what *that* meant.

Edward S. Ellis

Then the penetrating gaze outlined the figure of a man, sneaking like a wild animal, down the river bank. He was seen only faintly, but he was equally sure of *his* identity. It was Burkhardt, one of the hated white men that had poisoned the mind of his brother and caused him to forget he was a Murhapa, whose word should be sacred.

An exultant gleam came into the dusky face, as he stole forward in the same direction that the convict took. The action of the miscreant showed that he was following some prey, and who was it as likely to be as the white man that was abroad and was held in such detestation by the scoundrel?

Burkhardt, in one respect, acted precisely as did his intended victim. The latter was so absorbed in his own delicious thoughts, that, after that hurried glance around him, he did not once again look to the rear. So Burkhardt, never once dreaming that he was under surveillance, kept his gloating eyes fixed on the shadowy figure in front, without looking to see that while the man was hunting the tiger another tiger was not hunting him.

Being a slight distance to the rear of the convict, Ziffak could not see the form in front of him with equal distinctness, but the faint glimpse which he caught was all he needed.

Thus the strange procession passed up the western bank of the calmly flowing Xingu. Fred Ashman moving slowly and lost in reverie, Burkhardt prowling like a wild beast behind him, with Ziffak clinging to the heels of the wretch as if he were his very shadow.

The moon, which gave but faint light at the beginning, increased in power as the minutes passed. Ziffak fell back, so that if Burkhardt should look around, he would not recognize though he might see him.

But the ruffian did not turn his head: he was too intent on the fearful task before him.

Suddenly he stopped. Instantly Ziffak crouched down into the smallest possible space and clutched his javelin. The increasing moonlight showed that he had passed beyond the upper end of the village and was watching the lovers on the fringe of the forest beyond.

A movement on the part of Burkhardt, as if he were making preparation to fire his rifle, caused Ziffak to move swiftly and silently forward until he was within twenty paces. Then he paused, for he was close enough.

The change of position on the part of the pursuer enabled him to catch the outlines of the lovers, so absorbed in each other's presence that they forgot to keep within the sheltering shadow of the trees.

Burkhardt could ask for no better opportunity than that which was now before him. He knew the inextinguishable hatred of King Haffgo for this white man, and no greater favor could be done the ruler than to slay him.

Sinking on one knee, he carefully brought his gun to a level. The gleam of the moonlight on the barrel insured unerring aim.

But a moment before it was perfected, Ashman stepped forward and seized the hand of his adored one. This caused such a change of the relative situation of the two that the weapon could not be fired without endangering the life of the maiden.

That would never do, and waiting a moment in the hope that another charge would take place, Burkhardt began stealthily moving to the right to secure the advantage. A few steps up the slope were all that was required, when he again knelt on one knee and pointed his rifle at the unsuspicious American.

It was but an instant before that Ariel caught sight of the crouching figure and was transfixed with terror. The moonlight enabled her to identify the person, who was aiming his gun either at her or her companion.

Before she could speak, and at the moment Ashman turned his head, a giant figure was seen to rise as if out of the very earth, directly behind the miscreant. He held his prodigious javelin poised over his bead. He was seen to make a sudden onward movement and then the weapon vanished.

Speeding toward the couple with such amazing velocity it was invisible; but, ere the crouching convict could press the trigger of his rifle, he was seen to sprawl forward, his gun flying from his grasp. The terrible javelin had gone entirely through his body as though it were tissue paper, and pinned him like an impaled insect to the earth!

"The scoundrel!" exclaimed Ashman, who was just too late to anticipate their friend.

"It is Ziffak who has saved us!" gasped Ariel, shrinking against the side of her lover.

The herculean chieftain towered aloft in more imposing proportions than ever as he strode toward the startled couple. Whether he was advancing to regain his weapon, or whether he meant to join them could not be known; for, before he reached the body of the assassin, he abruptly stopped and looked in the direction of the village.

He had caught an ominous sound: it was that made by the discharge of firearms!

"Great heaven!" exclaimed Ashman; "they have attacked my friends in Ziffak's house; I must go to their help; dearest Ariel, what will become of you?" added the distracted lover.

"Leave me alone," she replied, becoming calm again; "I can return home."

"Well, then, good-bye! It may be for the last time," he impulsively added, catching her, his one arm clasped about her yielding form and drawing her to him. Then, while she only faintly resisted, he kissed her passionately, as a lover kisses the queen of his heart when he believes he is bidding her farewell forever.

Suddenly, Ashman felt both of the willowy arms about his own neck, and she returned his caresses with a fervor equal to his own.

"Heaven bless and keep you!" he murmured; "I now have everything to live for! I shall fight hard, for it is not the life of my friends or my own that it is at stake! It is *you*! It is YOU!"

The startled Ziffak had paused but an instant, when he read aright the meaning of the sounds of guns from the village. The explorers had been attacked by the Murhapas. King Haffgo must have given the order. He had violated his pledge for the first time in his life. Great was his provocation!

The bosom of the giant heaved with indignation. He stood glaring like a lion at the keepers who are torturing his mate to death, while he is barred within the cage and cannot rush

Edward S. Ellis

to her help.

Then, wheeling about, he broke into a run straight for his home, whence came the shots that left no doubt that Professor Grimcke, Jared Long, and perchance their servants were fighting for their lives.

The chieftain had not far to go, and half the distance was passed, when he paused as suddenly as he had started. A new and startling decision had formed itself in his mind.

Again he wheeled and dashed toward the spot where he had left the lovers a minute before.

They saw him coming, and Ashman released his beloved and started to join the chieftain, who he suspected had come for him.

"Back!" he commanded, waving his immense arms; "neither of you must go to the village!"

"But what shall we do?" asked Ariel, pausing in front of the excited giant.

"Flee at once! Delay not a moment! If you do not, Haffgo will slay both of you! They are searching for Ariel! They suspect she is with you! They will soon know it and death awaits each!"

CHAPTER XXVI

THE FLIGHT

Never had Ziffak shown such fearful excitement. He swung his arms, and in his wild agitation uttered some of his words in Murhapa, but his meaning was caught by Ashman, who was infected by his overwhelming emotion. He was distraught for the moment, and stood undecided what to do.

It was the lovely Ariel who showed the most self-command.

"Whither shall we go, Ziffak?" she asked in English.

"To the enchanted lake; to the burning mountain! You know the way! Nothing else will save you, and you are lost if you wait another minute!"

And laying hands on the young man, he whirled him about and gave him a shove which nearly threw him off his feet. Then he reached to catch her, but she eluded him and slipped like a bird to the side of her lover.

"We will go!" said she; "leave us alone!"

Ashman turned his head and seizing the hand of his companion, said,

Edward S. Ellis

"You are my guide now! Lead on, and I will follow you to the death!"

She made no answer, but moved rapidly through the wood until they came to the open space along the river. Here, since there were no obstructions, they increased their pace almost to a run. He sought to maintain his place beside her, but she moved so fast, with little apparent effort that it was hard to do so.

He had his Winchester and revolver, and he glanced behind to learn whether they were followed. Ziffak had vanished, and no one was in sight. It was well that such was the fact; for he would not have hesitated to shoot down any that might appear.

The extraordinary flight continued for a furlong, and then Ariel paused on the edge of the Xingu. Her lover saw the reason: a small canoe lay against the shore.

"Is this to be used?" he asked, glancing in her pale face.

She nodded her head, and, lifting her skirts, stepped daintily within, and sat down near the stern. He shoved the boat clear, sprang in and sat down near the middle, as he seized the broad thin paddle.

Although considerably above the rapids, which had been the cause of all his difficulty, Ashman noticed that the current was not so swift as that encountered at many places leagues below; and, since the width was no greater, it followed that that portion of the Upper Xingu was of unusual depth.

In the strange excitement of the occasion, the lovers spoke few words. They had said much, and, when the opportunity should again come, they would say a great deal more; but they were fleeing for their lives, and any distraction of their whole interest and effort was likely to be fatal.

Ariel realized this as fully as did Ashman. She continually glanced in every direction, especially toward the village which was fast receding behind them. Fred swung the paddle powerfully, but with as little noise as possible.

In such crises of a man's life he thinks rapidly. While the young man's heart was aglow with the ecstacy of a promised fulfillment of his love—a more glorious fulfillment than he had dared to dream of—he saw that a desperate struggle was not only certain but close at hand.

Very soon the flight of Ariel must be discovered, and her infuriated father would stop at nothing to punish the elopers. He could command hundreds of the most valiant warriors of the Matto Grosso, and any one, except such a lover as Fred Ashman, would have shrunk from the prodigious task before him.

When the flight of the canoe had continued for several minutes, and he could breathe a little more freely, he asked of his companion, whether she was familiar with the region they expected to visit.

The reply was singular. King Haffgo was accustomed to make regular excursions to the wonderful place, and he rarely did so without Ariel as his companion. He had guards stationed night and day to watch for the approach of strangers, for there was wealth enough to awaken the avarice even of the Emperor of Brazil himself.

Leaving his warriors at the entrance to the lake, with instructions to prevent any one following him, Haffgo would paddle the frail craft out upon the lake, with his daughter as his only companion.

They explored much of the strange locality, visiting places unknown, so far as they were aware, to every one else.

Ashman reflected that this was extremely fortunate so far as Ariel was concerned, for it gave her the very knowledge that was so necessary in their flight; but, unfortunately, their bitterest and most unrelenting enemy possessed the same knowledge.

Now the Xingu broadened, and the flow became still more moderate. Ashman held his paddle suspended and looked around.

"Are we entering the lake?"

"Not yet," she replied with a shake of her lovely head.

The oar was dipped again, and the light boat shot forward like a water fowl over the smooth surface.

He had noticed that the boat was similar to that used by Ziffak, being composed of a species of bark, the seams of which were skilfully joined with tendons, and the outside covered with a gum which rendered it close enough to exclude even air itself.

What seemed to be a creek a hundred feet wide, suddenly opened on the right, winding through an exuberant forest whose branches overhung the water. She motioned with her hand for him to guide the boat into this, adding that it was the entrance to the enchanted lake of which he had heard such glowing accounts, and whose existence, he remembered, had been denied by Ziffak, though it had been admitted by him only a brief while before.

The course of the canoe was changed, and Ashman involuntarily slackened the pace, while he gazed around with increasing wonder.

The distance was not far, when a towering rock was observed jutting out from the bank. It was fully twenty feet high, rough, jagged and massive and obtruded half-way across the stream.

She whispered to him to proceed as cautiously as he could, for on the rock was stationed one of the lookouts of King Haffgo, whose duty it was to challenge every one on his way to the enchanted lake. Ashman was told to keep his lips mute, in case they were hailed, as they were likely to be, and to leave to her any explanation it might be necessary to make.

In the bright moonlight, the sentinel was sure to notice the presence of a white man in the boat, but would be likely to believe he was either Waggaman or Burkhardt, while he would not dare to question the daughter of the king, however much he might be astonished at her presence at this time.

Ashman saw the figure of a Murhapa, but instead of being erect, he was seated on a ledge of the rock, his body half prone and in a motionless posture. The paddle was dipped more softly than ever as the craft came opposite him, but he did not speak, or stir.

"He's asleep?" whispered Ashman, looking inquiringly at her.

She nodded her head, and he did not require to be told of the great gain that would be secured, if they could pass without awaking him.

With that view, he used the utmost care, causing only the faintest ripple, as he propelled the light craft over the mirror-like surface.

In a few seconds, the massive rock was passed, and still the sentinel remained as motionless, as if he were a part of the solid stone, on which he was seated. He surely was a negligent servant to lose his consciousness thus early in the night.

A few more strokes, and a turn in the creek left him out of sight. *That* danger was safely passed, and Fred Ashman drew a sigh of relief, accepting it as a good omen of their future.

He now dipped the paddle deeper, and, within the following five minutes, the canoe and its occupants debouched upon the waters of the wonderful enchanted lake.

CHAPTER XXVII

SHUT IN

The situation in which the visitors to the dominions of King Haffgo were placed, was such as to sharpen their wits to the keenest edge.

After the departure of Fred Ashman, Ziffak talked more plainly with the Professor and New Englander. The head chieftain told his white friends what they had suspected; Haffgo was enraged at Ashman's presumption with his daughter. He was in that mood indeed, in which, but for his promise, he would have hurled his javelin at the youth before he left the audience chamber.

Ziffak, however, was hopeful that the anger of his royal brother would cool sufficiently to allow the visitors to remain there two days; but he doubted whether, after all, they would want to stay that long under the strained condition of things.

When the chieftain took his departure, it was without any hint that he wished to have an eye to the young gentleman, but Grimcke and Long suspected it, and their conversation became of the gravest character, for they fully realized their peril.

Edward S. Ellis

They regretted the mad infatuation of their young friend with Ariel the princess, and yet they did not blame him, for, as the New Englander remarked, could they have believed there was any hope for them, they would have fallen as irrestrainably in love as he.

But they did not, and, therefore, were in a frame of mind to consider the situation more coolly than the hot-headed lover.

Both agreed that the stroll taken by Ashman was likely to bring about trouble, but they were powerless to do anything. Ziffak was the only individual who could manage matters in such an emergency.

It will be remembered that night had fully come at the time of the chieftain's departure. The interior of the room would have been wrapped in gloom, had not the mother of Ziffak made her appearance and started a fire on the hearth at the further end of the apartment.

The white men watched her closely to see how the Murhapas were accustomed to secure ignition. But they were disappointed. She raked aside the ashes until some embers were disclosed beneath, which were readily fanned into a flame. This caused the apartment to shine with a light like that at mid-day.

She had brought in an earthen vessel of water and began broiling several thin slices of meat on the coals. They were quickly finished, and she then handed to each of her guests the prepared meat on an earthen plate. All ate heartily, using their fingers for knives and forks, while the cool water could not have been more refreshing.

Bippo and Pedros had been sleeping and resting so long that they desired to get out doors. Since they were not likely to be recognized in the night, if they used caution, Grimcke and Long told them to go, but to take care they did not lose themselves.

They had hardly departed when their hostess also left, passing out by the rear way. She did not speak, but as she was disappearing, gave the two men such a strange look that their suspicions were awakened. Both at that moment were reflecting upon the ominous news brought them by Ziffak.

By a common impulse, both hastened to the rear to learn all they could about the building in which they might be compelled to fight for their lives.

The result was rather pleasing. The structure was heavier and more compact than the ordinary buildings, and, in addition to the usual opening in front, had one at the rear, through which the woman undoubtedly passed on her way to her royal son.

Neither of these openings were provided with anything in the nature of a door that could be closed. Whenever the rare occasions arose for such a sealing of the inhabitants of a house, it was done by means of furs suspended in front of the entrance.

The white men noted this with quick eyes, and then went back to the front apartment.

"In the event of attack," said the Professor with the utmost coolness, "you can take the rear door and I the front."

Long nodded his head; he understood and was ready.

They had hardly entered the front apartment, when both were struck by the unusual chatter of voices on the outside. There must have been a large gathering of people who were growing excited about something.

The Professor was about to step into the opening to learn what it meant, when Bippo burst into the apartment, the picture of fright and terror.

"Going to kill us!" was his alarming exclamation; "make me run—almost kill me!"

"Where's Pedros?" asked Long.

"He scared—run into woods—won't come back—run all way to Am'zon!"

"I think he'll have to stop once or twice to get breath before he reaches there," was the characteristic comment of the Professor, who standing near the door, listened more closely to the threatening words and exclamations on the outside.

It sounded singular to recognize more than one expression uttered in English by these people, who, until a few years before were unaware that such people were living.

But for the proof Ziffak had given of his loyalty the whites might have connected his absence with the ugly signs outside; but the confidence even of Jared Long in his friendship was unshaken.

"Bippo," said the Professor, speaking with the same quiet self-possession he had shown in the first place, "they are going to attack us; more than likely we shall be killed, but there is a chance for you, because you are dressed like these people, and, so long as you can keep in the shadow, you can pass for one of them; you can slip out by the opening at the rear without being noticed; steal away, find Pedros if you can, and leave."

The eyes of the servant seemed to protrude from his head, as he grasped the fearful meaning of these words. Then, clutching his spear in his hand, he whisked like a shadow into the rear apartment beyond sight.

Grimcke and Long smiled in each other's face; they could not blame the fellow for thinking of his own safety.

"The music will begin in a few minutes," added the Professor. "I think you had better guard the rear; you understand, Jared, that it's no time to throw away any powder."

"I don't propose to waste my ammunition," muttered the New Englander, as he stepped softly into the rear apartment.

Only a slight reflection from the fire on the hearth found its way into that part of the house, which had no window; but by the dim light Jared Long saw a dusky figure come rapidly from the door toward him. He was on the point of raising his gun, when it spoke:

"It's me—Bippo."

"I thought you had left. Why didn't you go?"

"Love my white folks—can't leave 'em, stay die wid 'em."

This sounded very fine, but the New Englander was incredulous. He believed that their servant was more afraid to leave than to stay. He had probably taken a look outside and decided that he was safer under the shelter of those three Winchesters (for the weapon of poor Aaron Johnston was still in the possession of his friends).

Long was inclined to ask him to take charge of the extra rifle, and use it in helping to defend themselves; but,

Edward S. Ellis

recalling the antipathy of the fellow against handling firearms, he decided that he would only throw away his cartridges.

He, therefore, cautioned him to keep out of the reach of any of the missiles that were likely to come flying into the apartment, and urged him, in case he saw any opening, to dart out among the people and do his best to escape.

Professor Grimcke firmly believed that the impending fight would be to the death, and that the only issue would be the slaying of himself and companion. It was the same danger they had faced many times, with the difference that this was to be the last.

He surveyed his surroundings, like a general making ready to receive the assault of a foe, and die fighting in the last ditch.

There was the door in front and the two windows, through which the attack could be made. He could cover all three with his repeating rifle, and, when the last struggle came, appeal to his revolver and knife. He smiled, grimly at the reflection, that he had every ground for believing, that the victory of the Murhapas would prove the most costly they had ever won. Jared Long was his equal in markmanship and coolness, and, as he coolly remarked, there would be no ammunition wasted, by either.

CHAPTER XXVIII

BESIEGERS AND BESIEGED

Suddenly a bushy bead, with a black face, horribly distorted by passion, appeared at the window furthest from where Professor Grimcke was standing.

The right hand was raised and in the act of poising a javelin to hurl at the white man; but the latter, with an incredibly quick movement, brought his Winchester to a level and fired.

The bronze skull was shattered as though it were a rotten apple, and the Murhapa, with a resounding shriek, went backward in the darkness.

A slight rustling at the other window drew the white man's attention thither, and, without lowering his weapon, he let fly at a group who were simply peering within, evidently believing there was no call to use their javelins.

Another screech told that the bullet had found its mark, and the other faces vanished.

Then Grimcke stepped out from the wall to gain a view of the opening which answered for a door. A rustling there told him a crowd were gathering, but they had taken warning just

Edward S. Ellis

in time to avoid a third shot. Then he slipped a couple more cartridges from his belt into the magazine, so as to keep it full, and awaited the next step in this extraordinary business.

"I've about a hundred left," he reflected, "and that's enough to keep things on a jump, if I can dodge their javelins."

Meanwhile, Jared Long was not idle. He had but the opening at the rear to watch, and he did the duty well. Almost at the moment that his comrade fired his first shot, he descried the figure of a Murhapa trying to steal into the apartment without detection; but just enough of the moonlight that was shut from the front doors and windows, reached the rear of the building, to disclose the outlines of the head and shoulders, as he began stealthily creeping into the building.

Bippo had discovered the peril at the same moment, and clutched the arm of his master with a nervous intensity of terror. Long impatiently shook him off, and, with the same cool quickness of Professor Grimcke, drove a bullet through the head of the dusky miscreant, who was slain so suddenly that he rolled convulsively backward, without any outcry.

Almost at the same instant, a second native emitted a wild shout. He was directly behind the first and the latter lurched against him, causing such fright that he leaped back several feet with the involuntary cry fully understood by all whose ears it reached.

Long stood as rigid as a statue for several minutes, waiting for another chance, but none presented. Then he reflected that his position was much more favorable than Grimcke's, for not only had he but the single opening to guard, but his apartment was so shrouded in gloom that the sharpest-eyed warrior could not locate him from the outside.

The New Englander stepped to the door communicating with the front apartment and, barely showing himself, spoke:

"I can attend to the window on the right, Professor; leave that to me, while you watch the door and the other one."

"Thanks," returned his friend; "I think there is a little too much light in this part of the house."

Moving quickly to the hearth he heaped the ashes with his foot upon the blazing embers, until they were so smothered that only a few tiny twists of flame struggled through the covering. This left the place in such darkness that a sense of security instantly came to him.

"Good!" called the New Englander, who could no longer be discerned; "that makes matters more nearly equal!"

Although, as we have said, the moonlight was substantially shut off from the front of the heavy structure, yet the moon itself, being full, so illumined the surroundings that it was quite easy to distinguish the head and figure of any one of their enemies the instant he presented himself at one of the openings.

What both the defenders feared was, that the savages would make a sudden rush and force themselves within the cabin in spite of the disastrous reception they were sure to be given. Such an essay was certain to result in the overthrow of the whites, but the Murhapas must have realized the cost it would be to them. Brave as they were, they hesitated to incur the consequences until other means had failed.

Professor Ernest Grimcke now did a most daring thing. The fierce welcome he had given the attacking Murhapas resulted in their temporary demoralization. Knowing they would speedily recover, he decided to take advantage of the panic by an attempt to intensify it.

Striding to the door he paused on the very threshold and peered out upon the large space in his field of vision.

Fully a hundred savages were in sight. Apparently they had been crowding around the entrance when the shots from within caused a hasty scattering. They had halted a dozen yards or so away, where they were talking excitedly, still frightened and enraged, and with no thought of relinquishing the fight.

They had withdrawn so far from the front of the building that they were in the strong moonlight, and consequently in full view of the white man, who saw others of the natives hurrying from the right and left. Among them were women and children and the confusion and excitement were fearful.

Standing thus, Grimcke again raised his repeater and deliberately opened fire on the crowd. It seemed cruel, but it was an act of self-defence, for those people were clamoring for the lives of the two men within, and would not be satisfied until they were at their mercy.

It was a strange scene that followed. The interior of the building being dark, while the moonlight failed to touch the front, the figure of the white man was invisible to the dusky wretches howling on the outside.

All at once, from the black opening of the building, came the crash of the repeating Winchester. Spouts of fire shot out into the gloom in terrific succession, as if fiery serpents were darting their heads in different directions; for the marksman aimed, quickly to the right, to the left and to the front, never pausing until he had discharged half a score of shots.

The panic for a minute or two was indescribable. Men, women and children shrieked and scattered for the nearest available shelter. Behind the buildings and down the river bank they dashed, stumbled and rolled, until, but for the tragic nature of the scene, the white man would have smiled.

But he had done enough, and he stepped back within the room to replenish the magazine of his rifle.

Jared Long had been drawn into the room by the furious fusillade, and now put the startling question whether advantage could not be taken of the panic to make a sudden dash for the woods. It would never do to make for the boat still resting against the shore, for it would be filled with poisoned javelins before they could shove out into the Xingu.

"I believe we can," replied the Professor; "it will take them some minutes to get over their panic and that will be enough for us."

"Let us leave by the rear," said Long, "for I don't think that is so well guarded."

The two turned to attempt the dash for freedom, when a cry from Bippo struck them.

"Stay here," exclaimed the New Englander, fearing that a diversion was on foot; "and I'll attend to him!"

He was back in the apartment in an instant. The light on the hearth having been extinguished, the gloom in this portion of the building was impenetrable, but a fearful struggle of some kind was going on. Some animal or person had got within and grappled Bippo who was fighting like a tiger.

Had the New Englander been able to distinguish the combatants, he would have ended the contest in a twinkling, but though the two rolled against his feet, he dared not fire through fear of hurting his friend.

"Are you under or on top?" he asked, bending downward at the moment he knew from the peculiar sounds the foes had become stationary.

"*He on top*," was the doleful response.

Long extended his right hand to learn precisely how matters stood, or rather lay, when it came in contact with the arm of a Murhapa in the act of raising it aloft to bury his knife in the body of the helpless Bippo, who was at the mercy of the savage, holding him inextricably in his grasp.

The American secured a firm hold of the forearm, and with a powerful wrench, not only jerked the miscreant free, but flung him from one side of the room clean to the door, where he was visible in the faint light beyond.

Evidently concluding that his mission in that place was over, he nimbly came to his feet and shot like a rocket through the opening.

The New Englander was in no mood for sentimentality, and, he levelled his weapon with the intention to kill; but quick as he was, he was just a fraction of a minute too late, and, much to his chagrin, the dusky wretch got away unharmed.

Long darted into the front room, ready for the proposal he had made just before.

The Professor was peering out, seemingly debating whether it was not advisable to re-open his bombardment.

"It beats creation," he remarked, as his friend appeared at his elbow, "how quickly those fellows rally; their heads are popping up in every direction, and it won't do to try to steal out this way."

"But I suggested the rear," reminded Long.

"Let's see how matters look there."

The survey from the other opening was disappointing. Although all the Murhapas had been affected in a greater or less degree by the panic, yet it was more incomplete at the rear, because the confusing volley had not come from that direction.

There seemed to be fully as many warriors on this side, which, with the exception of the river, was quite similar in appearance to the other. The shadowy figures were observed moving noiselessly in a dozen different directions, their heads bent down and their bodies crouching, as if in expectation of a shot, but, at the same time, they were not to be frightened off by any fusilade from within.

"We're just too late," remarked the Professor, quick to take in every point of the situation; "we might have done it a minute ago, but they are watching too closely now."

"Let's open again," suggested the New Englander.

"Better wait awhile; they can be stampeded easier then than now," was the reply of the Professor.

During this lull, when it may be said the defenders were becoming accustomed to the siege, they had time to give a few minutes' thought to their absent friends, Fred Ashman and Ziffak, regarding whom it was natural to feel great curiosity.

They believed themselves warranted in hoping for the best, so far as Ashman was concerned. He had probably strolled some distance, and must have been warned by the firing of the Professor's Winchester from the front, of the serious danger in which his friends were involved. If all had gone well with the youth up to that time, he ought to be wise enough to get away without an instant's delay. What was feared was, that in his anxiety to help his comrades, he would run into a peril from which he could not extricate himself.

The real hope for the youth was centered on Ziffak. Believing he had gone forth to look after Ashman, they were confident he would speedily get upon his track. If so, he would not permit him to return to the village.

From what the reader has been told, it will be seen that the defenders were not far off in their conjectures.

But, when they came to speculate upon the part that the head chieftain was likely to take, affecting Grimcke and Long, they were all at sea. It would ever be a source of wonder that he had been transformed from a relentless enemy into the strongest of friends, but they fully realized that such friendship must have its bounds.

Ziffak might not shrink from using very plain speech when talking face to face with his brother, but it was hardly to be supposed that he would raise his arm against his authority. At the time Ziffak made known the probability that the explorers might be compelled to take their departure that evening, he gave no intimation of any purpose of helping them to resist such an order.

Accustomed as he was to lead the warlike Murhapas in battle, he might well hesitate to ask them to turn their weapons against the king, and if he should presume on such treason, all the probabilities were that such weapons would be turned against the head chieftain himself.

Edward S. Ellis

CHAPTER XXIX

ACROSS THE LAKE

A few minutes after passing the bend in the stream, which hid the rock and the sleeping sentinel from sight, Fred Ashman observed that the smooth current broadened into a lake, forming the extraordinary sheet of water of which he had heard such strange accounts.

He held the paddle suspended, and looked around.

The surface was as calm as the face of a mirror, and in the strong moonlight, as he looked down he could see that it was of crystalline clearness—so much so, indeed, that a boat or any floating object looked as if suspended in mid-air.

It expanded right and left and in front, until he could barely discern the dim outlines of trees and rocks that shut it in. It was probably two or three square miles in extent, and to the westward the shore appeared to be composed of enormous boulders and masses of rocks.

Directly ahead, was a crag more massive than the rest, towering a hundred feet above the lake, with a breadth fully one half as great. It resembled some gigantic sentinel, keeping ward and watch over the strange region unknown to few if any white man.

Ashman turned to his companion with the question, what course he should take, and, without speaking, she pointed to the rock which she saw had attracted his attention.

Very slight effort was required to propel the delicate craft, which seemed to become sentient, and to move forward in obedience to the wishes of its occupants. He barely dipped the blade into the water, when it skimmed forward like a swallow. After a number of strokes he ceased and fixed his eyes on the landmark by which he was proceeding.

A singular emotion held him speechless for the time. The vast mass of stone appeared to be slowly rising from the bosom of the lake, and, instead of remaining motionless, was advancing to meet the tiny canoe and its awed occupants. One moment, it was like some vast ogre, stealing silently about to crush them beneath the clear waters, and then it became a friendly giant, reaching out its hand to lead them forward.

But for the distant sounds of firing at the Murhapa village, Fred Ashman would have felt that it was all a vision of sleep, from which he must soon awake to the realities of life.

But that horrible, grinding discord continually creeping into their ears told too plainly the dreadful scenes at comparatively a short distance. Even in his exalted mental state, Ashman began to ask himself what was to be the end of the strange venture upon which he had started. A disquieting misgiving arose, that perhaps he had not done the wisest thing in leaving his imperilled friends.

But he reflected that he had only obeyed the orders of Ziffak, who indeed would not have permitted his wishes to be disregarded, for who should know the wisest course so well as he? Besides, his own reason told him that if the Professor and his companion were attacked in the cabin, it was impossible for him to raise a finger in their behalf.

And so he dismissed that phase of the marvellous business from his mind and faced the present situation.

He had fled with Ariel from her father, King Haffgo. Instead of turning to the northward down the Xingu, they had gone further up the stream and directly away from the right course out of the perilous country.

But while, in one sense, this might be looked upon as the height of recklessness, he saw it was unavoidable. Had they turned down the Xingu, there would have been no escaping their foes, while the enchanted lake and its surroundings must afford secure shelter for a time.

But for how long?

That was the question which obtruded itself, even while filled with the delightful thrill of his new love, and when *en rapport* with his marvellous surroundings.

The intimate knowledge which Ariel possessed of the region would guide them to some spot where they could reasonably hope to be safe from pursuit, unless such pursuit was led by her enraged parent.

Ashman was still scrutinizing the great mass of rock, steadily assuming more definite shape in the moonlight as the intervening distance decreased, when he was surprised that he had not noticed the mountainous elevation behind it. The immense rock seemed but the beginning of others rising beyond to the height of a thousand feet, while they broadened to the right and left until they stretched over an extent of several miles.

It seemed to him that these constituted a spur of the Geral range, which extend in a northwesterly direction between the Guapore River (forming a part of the eastern boundary of Bolivia) and the headwaters of the Tapajos and Xingu. If so, their extent was continuous for a hundred miles.

Ashman had ceased paddling, though, under the faint momentum remaining, the canoe continued slowly moving over the lake and gradually drawing near the rock. He did not break the silence, but asked himself what could be the reason of Ariel's direction for him to paddle toward the rock. He supposed there was some place of concealment which she had in mind, though he discerned nothing of that nature.

"We cannot stay there forever," was the practical thought in the mind of the lover, who felt the next moment as though he would be happy to dwell forever anywhere with her.

"After we have staid here until pursuit is given up—*if it ever will be*—then we must leave the country. I will take her to my home in North America, where I shall love and cherish her and become the envied of all men."

"We are approaching the rock," he said, addressing her; "what next, dearest Ariel."

"Paddle right on," was the astonishing reply.

He looked at her with a questioning smile. Could she be in earnest?

"Right on," she repeated, reading his thoughts aright.

Edward S. Ellis

"Very well; the slave obeys his mistress," he replied, giving the paddle another dip in the water.

Gazing ahead, he instantly discovered the cause of her reply. A tunnel opened into the rock, seemingly near the centre. It was perhaps ten feet in height and with a width slightly greater. Could it be she meant he should enter that black forbidding passage? He asked the question and she replied that such was her wish.

He could not decline to take her whither she desired to go. Gently swaying the blade, he sent the boat within the dark opening, which appeared to distend its jaws to swallow the canoe and them from the world to which they had bidden good-bye.

Ashman was beginning to ask himself how he was to continue the advance in the darkness, which must become impenetrable as they passed beyond the limit of the moon-light, when he perceived the water into which he dipped the paddle.

Not only that, but it grew more distinct as he progressed, until once more the form of his beloved came out to view, as she sat near him in the canoe.

Wondering what it all meant, he gazed ahead. The surface of the water grew plainer, as his eye ranged along the tunnel, until, only a short distance away, the view was clearer than on the lake itself, beneath the full moon.

What was the explanation of this wonderful sea of illumination into which he was guiding the canoe?

CHAPTER XXX

A GUESS

Standing in the door of the building, his figure so wrapped in gloom that it was invisible to the fierce Murhapas, Professor Grimcke cautiously peered out upon the multitude that were clamorously seeking the death of himself and comrade.

The horde seemed to be everywhere. They were glaring over the river bank, behind which they could find secure shelter by merely dropping their heads; they were crouching at the corners of the adjacent houses, the king's residence affording screen to fully a score. Not yet fully recovered from their panic, they appeared to be awaiting the leadership of some strong man who held the fire-arms of the explorers in less dread than they.

A form rose upright along the Xingu, at the upper portion of the line of savages. In the full moonlight he was as clearly revealed as if at mid-day.

It was with strange feelings that Professor Grimcke saw that this individual belonged to the same race as himself. He was one of the two white men that had lived for years among the Murhapas and who had instigated the furious assault upon them.

Edward S. Ellis

"You have earned your fate," muttered the German, bringing his unerring Winchester once more to his shoulder, and sighting as best he could at the unconscious miscreant, who appeared to be conversing with some one sitting on the ground at his side.

The finger of Grimcke was pressing the trigger when, yielding to an unaccountable impulse, he lowered the weapon. He was impatient with himself that his heart should fail him at the critical moment, but perhaps it was well it was so.

"You and I ought to be friends," he reflected, "and it is not my fault that we are not, however, I cannot shoot you down like a dog, though you deserve it."

The emotion which checked him so unexpectedly, also prevented his renewing fire upon the Murhapas, who were really less guilty than he.

He had decided to await the next demonstration before discharging his gun again.

Jared Long was as vigilant and alert as his friend. It may be doubted whether he would have spared Waggaman, had he been given the opportunity to draw bead on him. He realized too vividly that the two defenders never would have been in this fearful situation but for the machinations of those two men.

It seemed to him that Bippo was curiously quiet. He had not spoken, nor, so far as he could judge, moved since his own return from his brief conference with the Professor.

He pronounced his name in a low voice, but there was no reply. A call in a louder tone also failed of response.

"I wonder whether he was killed?" was the thought which led Long to leave his station at the door, and to set out on a tour of investigation around the room, using his hands and feet to aid him.

He expected every minute to come in contact with the lifeless figure of his helper, whom he supposed to have been pierced by the poisoned weapon of the Murhapa; but when he had passed around the apartment and across it several times, until assured that not a foot of square space had been neglected he awoke to the fact that Bippo was not there.

It was hardly probable that he had entered the front apartment, but he made inquiry of the Professor. The latter replied that he had heard nothing of him; but, since he had a few minutes that could be spared without danger for that purpose, he went through a search similar to that of his friend.

"He is not here," called the Professor, in a guarded undertone.

The surprising conclusion followed that the fellow after all had effected his escape from the building, though how it was done puzzled the two whom he left behind.

Bippo had got away by yielding to one of those sudden inspirations which sometimes come to a person. Hearing the explorers speaking about a stealthy withdrawal by the rear, he decided to anticipate them. Without pausing to debate the matter or ask for permission, he slipped out the rear door and moved rapidly off in a crouching posture.

He must have been seen by numbers of the Murhapas, but was mistaken for one of their own number.

The error cannot be regarded as remarkable, when it is recalled that Bippo bore a strong resemblance to the savages around them. He was dressed the same and carried a spear similar to the missiles used by them. Though he lacked their bushy heads and stature, these were not marked enough to attract notice at a time when the Murhapas knew that several of their number had been defeated in their efforts to enter the structure from the rear.

With his wits sharpened by his danger, Bippo displayed admirable discretion. Showing no undue haste or flurry, he avoided too close acquaintance with the savages, who were so absorbed in the work of securing the destruction of the white men that they paid less attention to such an incident than they would at any other time.

So it was that he edged farther and farther away, until he found himself so close to the woods that he whisked among the trees without any one questioning or trying to check him. He was free at last, and, as if Dame Fortune had decided to take him in charge, he had hardly reached the margin of the Xingu, at a point considerably below the village, when he almost stumbled over Pedros, who was waiting and wondering what he ought to do next.

Both the Professor and his friend were glad that Bippo had managed to get away. They liked the fellow, and, even if they must be sacrificed, it was a relief to know that the poor native, who had had such a woful experience since leaving the Amazon, now had a fighting chance of escaping from the dreadful region.

Besides, as has been shown, the presence of the fellow was more of an incumbrance than a help. But for the delay caused by Long's rush to his help, the whites would have made a dash for liberty themselves, though the question of their escape was problematical to the last degree.

Precious little ground could the explorers see for extricating themselves from their peril. The Murhapas numbered a hundred, all were brave, and the weapons in their hands were dreaded tenfold more than firearms. It seemed miraculous that Grimcke and Long had not been pierced long before. Why did not the Murhapas set fire to the building, after the manner of the North American Indians?

This was the question which both the defenders had asked themselves several times, but in the case of each the answer was obvious.

The house, it will be recalled, adjoined that of King Haffgo, and, although there was no wind blowing, the burning of the less important structure was sure to endanger the other. As a last resort, the white men might be driven out in that way, but not yet.

If the besiegers could persuade themselves to make a united rush, they would be sure to prevail; but, as has been explained, the cost of such an essay was sure to be frightful, and led the Murhapas to defer that, also, until assured less risky means would not prevail.

It seemed to our friends that there were scores of schemes which ought to be successful, and, such being the case, it will be understood why they believed their last fight was on, and why they were disposed to show no mercy to their assailants.

The Professor was surprised, knowing, as he did, the part taken against them by Waggaman and Burkhardt, that no reports of firearms had yet been heard among the assailants. It would seem as if something of the kind was required in

Edward S. Ellis

order that those miscreants should retain their prestige among the people.

Now, all these thoughts and many more passed through the minds of the defenders in a tenth of the time it has taken us to put them on paper. It was yet early in the evening, and the crisis in the siege must come before long.

Jared Long peeped out of the rear entrance. A study of what he saw showed little change in the situation. He was convinced that the next demonstration would be from the front. He, therefore, did not hesitate to leave his post and slip into the next room for a few hasty words with the Professor.

"There's no use of staying in here," he said, "for we are sure to be overwhelmed within the next hour."

"I fully agree with you."

"And I can see but one desperate hope."

"What is that?"

"To follow Bippo."

"I agree with you again; let us make such a demonstration from the front that we shall be able to draw most of them there; then one of us will make a rush."

"Why not both."

"We shall fail; one must keep up the firing while they think both are at it, and then the other can make the attempt."

"Very well; let me open here."

"No; we will both do it; you know that this station is mine and as soon as there appears to be a chance, you can make the start."

Now, both of the men believed in their hearts that if the desperate scheme could work, that the utmost it could do would be to save one: there could be no earthly chance for the other.

It was characteristic of the chivalrous friendship of each that he had fully determined that that forlorn opportunity should be given to the other.

But they understood their mutual natures too well to waste any words in argument, for neither would yield.

"Very well, Professor; we'll draw lots."

"I will agree to that."

It was so dark in the room that they could not see each other, nor did either window afford light enough for their purpose.

Grimcke glanced out the door. No immediate movement seemed impending, and they moved to the fire-place. The Professor kicked some of the ashes aside and a tiny blaze arose, throwing a dull illumination over a few feet of the room.

The Professor drew an American coin from his pocket,—one that he had kept ever since entering South America.

"Now," said he, placing both hands behind his back, "tell me which contains it."

"The right," said the New Englander.

Edward S. Ellis

"You have lost," coolly replied the Professor, bringing the two hands quickly to the front and opening the palms.

Sure enough the coin was in the left, but the sly fellow did not confess that he had deftly changed it after his companion made his guess.

CHAPTER XXXI

A DESPERATE SCHEME

Not another word was said. The question had been submitted to the arbitrament of chance and the New Englander had lost, and that, too without any suspicion on his part of the little trick played upon him.

Before resorting to the last opportunity, Long slipped through the back room and ascertained the outlook there. He was surprised at the result. Hardly a native was visible. It looked indeed as if they were working their way round to the front, and that some scheme of attack had been agreed upon by the leaders from that point.

The Professor's survey confirmed the theory of his friend. The Murhapas were more plentiful than ever. They appeared to be marshalling along the bank of the Xingu, where there were so many that it was impossible to count the heads and shoulders rising above the slope.

Waggaman was not in sight, though there could be no doubt that he was the inspiring spirit in the movement. All the indications were that a rush had been agreed upon. Should it be permitted to come off unopposed in its incipiency, it would be all up with the men who had defended themselves so bravely thus far.

"I will begin at the head of the row," said the Professor, "and you at the foot; make every shot tell."

"All right; begin!"

The fusillade was opened the same instant. Both men fired rapidly, and, though they could not pause to make their aim as sure as they wished, and though it is not to be supposed that every shot was effective, yet the execution was dreadful.

Arms were seen flung spasmodically upwards, figures leaped clear off the ground and then fell back out of sight, shrieks and shouts filled the air, and still the crack of the Winchesters continued without intermission.

One gratifying feature of the fearful scene was that the warriors began flocking around to the front, though they kept well back, as if to avoid the murderous discharge. These new arrivals not only afforded additional targets to the riflemen, despite their furious efforts to screen themselves, but proved that the scheme of the defenders was working as they desired: the natives were swarming from the rear to the front.

"Off with you; don't wait!" commanded the Professor.

"Good-bye!" was all that Jared Long said, as he darted from the side of his gallant friend and vanished.

Professor Grimcke took a few seconds to refill his magazine, when up went his Winchester again and the furious discharges seemed to be more rapid than before.

It would naturally be supposed that if the assailants saw that both of the white men had concentrated their fusillade at the front, they would make a dash to the rear. That, it may be said, would be the second step in the programme. It was calculated that the sudden volleys of the rifles would draw all the natives thither, and then, after learning what had taken place, a large part of them would rush back again.

The New Englander had been gone only a few minutes, when the Professor saw evidences that the second step was about to be taken. The savages were beginning to move back to the rear, though at a greater distance then from the building than before.

All at once Grimcke ceased firing. While looking sharply out of the door, he mechanically refilled the magazine of his rifle from his stock of cartridges which was running low.

"Now or never!" he said to himself, and then, turning, he ran swiftly through the two rooms to the rear door, through which he bounded without a moment's hesitation.

He expected his flight would be announced by a series of shouts and a storm of poisoned javelins. He held his breath, and, as the seconds passed, began wondering whether there was a possibility after all of successfully following the footsteps of his friend.

He was encouraged by the sounds of the deafening tumult from the front of the house. The Murhapas had swarmed into the front-room, proving that they had decided upon making the very rush of which the defenders stood in such dread.

This, although only a momentary diversion, was immeasurably in favor of the daring attempt of the flying fugitive.

Lest the reader may pronounce the escape of these two white men incredible, we hasten to explain that which, if left unexplained, would warrant such disbelief on the part of our friends.

The individual who gave the wild scheme an ending that otherwise it never could have had, was Ziffak, the head chieftain of the Murhapas. He proved to be the all-potent factor in the terrible problem.

From what has been related about these strange inhabitants of the Matto Grosso, it need not be said that they were too cunning, if left to themselves, to allow a door to stand open for their intended victims to escape, after penning them in such a trap.

Ziffak was the shrewdest member of the Murhapa tribe and much more fitted to be its ruler than King Haffgo. After bidding good-bye to the lovers, he hastened back to the middle of the village, where he arrived after the first disastrous repulse given his people by Professor Grimcke.

It took the fellow but a few moments to grasp the situation. He told no one of the death of Burkhardt, but busied himself in learning precisely how matters stood. Had he dared to do so, he would have ordered a cessation of the attack, but the latter was made by the direct orders of King Haffgo, and Ziffak was not the chieftain to butt his head against a stone wall, by an open defiance of his royal brother's authority.

The assault was under the direction of Waggaman himself. The king from his own door, where he could not be reached by any bullet of the defenders, was watching the futile assault with an impatience and anger that could hardly be restrained. His soul became like a volcano, as he saw his brave warriors fall back, with many of them biting the dust. Had not the traditions of his country forbade such a proceeding, he would have placed himself at the head of the natives and led the decisive charge.

Seeing how it was at the front, Ziffak cautiously made his way to the rear. There were few warriors there, and he instinctively felt that if his white friends were to get off at all, it must be through the rear opening.

While intently debating with himself what he could do to help them, he stealthily slipped down to where the large boat was lying under the bank. No one was near it, for the attention of all was concentrated on the fight under way. Unobserved, he shoved the craft out into the stream and saw it drift with the current.

Returning to the rear of the besieged building again, he formed the plan of getting the warriors to the front and then dashing back and helping them out. This was a wild scheme, and involved great personal risk to himself, for he was sure to be punished for rendering aid whose discovery was inevitable.

At the very moment he was about to make the attempt, Grimcke and Long gave him unexpected help by opening their united fire from the front upon the warriors marshalling for the decisive charge.

This afforded him just the pretext he wanted, to order the Murhapas to hasten to the other side of the building to assist in what was in contemplation there, though, even with such a movement under way, it will be seen that the right place for a portion of the savages was at the rear, in order to head off the very thing that was attempted.

Thus it was, that, while the two explorers were congratulating themselves on the success of their clever scheme, they never suspected that its success was due to their giant friend, who kept himself so well in the background that neither of them caught sight of him.

Having got his men away, Ziffak slipped back with the purpose of carrying out the rest of the plan he had formed; but before he could reach the rear entrance, he caught sight of Professor Grimcke running like a deer toward the woods.

Ziffak was puzzled, not knowing that his friend had preceded him, and he dashed into the building to hurry him out. As he came in at one door, Waggaman and the Murhapas swarmed in at the other, and pandemonium was let loose.

The certainty of another murderous fire from the rifles of the defenders caused some lagging at the threshold, but those in the rear forced those at the front forward, and the next moment the mob was inside.

Still there was no sound of firearms, though, the savages were crowding into both apartments. Some one kicked the ashes from the embers, and the blaze which followed made known the astounding fact that both of the white men had fled.

Ziffak seemed to be in a towering rage because such a blunder had been made, and called upon the fleetest runners to follow him.

Out of the door he went as if shot from the throat of a columbiad, with a procession of sinewy-limbed warriors at his heels. All ran as fast as they could, though none were his equal in fleetness.

It need hardly be said that Ziffak took mighty good care that he did not pursue the course of Professor Grimcke, and presumably that of his companion who preceded him.

Instead of aiming for the woods, he diverged toward the river, and seemed to find it necessary to shout and yell every second or two at the top of his voice.

His followers may have imagined he was laboring under uncontrollable rage or deemed it necessary to keep their courage up to the highest point by such means; but the two fugitives who had joined each other in the woods, and were picking their way with the utmost care, held a strong suspicion that the prodigious shouts were intended for their special benefit. At any rate, they accepted them as such, and took pains to continue their flight in a different course from that of the howling Murhapas.

It did not require Ziffak long to find out that the fugitives were irrecoverably gone, and he came back with his report to the king.

There he was met by astounding news. Burkhardt had been slain by a poisoned javelin, and Ariel, the beloved daughter of the ruler, had been seen in full flight toward the enchanted lake in the company of the execrated white man, Ashman. Pursuit was to be organized at once, and, though Ziffak was to take part, yet the chosen warriors were to be led by the king in person.

CHAPTER XXXII

THE BURNING MOUNTAIN

The tunnel through which Ashman propelled the canoe containing himself and Ariel, was more than a hundred yards in length. It was only for the smallest distance that the craft was in darkness, when the water began to reflect light and reveal its outlines.

A few minutes later the tunnel was passed, and they debouched into an expansion of the enchanted lake. The second division was similar to the other and almost as large, but its appearance was tenfold more wonderful.

The sheet of water may be said to have been divided into two nearly equal parts by the narrow tunnel running under the mass of rocks described. One division was in the outer air, after the usual fashion of lakes, while the other was wholly underground.

The interior lake was nearly circular in shape, with an arching roof hundreds of feet high. It was surrounded by towering crags, and volcanic masses of stone, which gave it an appearance different from anything on which Fred Ashman had ever looked. Nothing grander, wilder, more picturesque or romantic can be conceived. It was a scene which an explorer could stand for hours and contemplate in rapt admiration.

But the most amazing feature of this underground lake was the way in which it was illuminated, so that every portion stood out in as bold relief as if under the flaming sun of midday.

At the western side, the shore, as was the case in nearly all other directions, was a mass of jagged rocks, piled upon each other in the wildest confusion. Beyond these rocks, was a vast chasm above the level of the lake, and extending right and left for a distance of fifty rods. This huge chasm was one mass of crimson light, whose rays pierced every nook and cranny on every side of the lake.

The eye gazing in that direction saw something similar to that which greets the traveller in the far north, when viewing the play of the aurora borealis in the horizon, or when the red sun is rising from its ocean bed.

This enormous opening was so surcharged with light that Ashman, after contemplating it but a minute or two, did not need to ask its source. Beyond the area of illumination was the burning mountain whose blood-red glow covered the entire surface and shores of the underground portion of the enchanted lake. The volcano had been aflame for ages, and was likely to continue to burn for centuries to come.

Such an eternal conflagration must have an outlet for the vast quantity of vapor generated, and Ashman wondered that he had not noticed the ascending smoke on his way thither. He recalled that when he and his friend were coming up the Xingu, far below the last rapids, they observed a dark cloud resting in the western horizon. There was no thought at that time that it was caused by a burning mountain, but such must have been the fact. The most singular fact was, that while on his way across the lake to the tunnel, he had failed to notice and remark it.

There was a steady draft in the direction of the flaming cavern. He had observed it while paddling through the tunnel where it was strong enough to assist in the propulsion of the canoe. It was caused by the ascent of the vapor through the chimney of the fiery mountain, and averted the intolerable heat that otherwise would have been felt over every portion of the lake. As it was, a moderate increase of temperature was perceptible.

Ashman was tempted to paddle the canoe to the black rocks which separated the chasm from the lake, and he timidly moved the blade, restrained by the fear of something in the nature of a "back draft," which might consume them before they could escape.

Ariel assured him that she had never encountered or heard of anything of the kind, though she had often visited this remarkable region in the company of her father. Thereupon Ashman sent the boat ahead faster than before, and a minute later the bow touched the rocky wharf.

Stepping out, he drew the bow upon the rocks, so as to hold it fast, and, extending his hand, assisted her to shore. Then he drew the craft still further up, and, taking her hand again in his own, began picking their way over the jagged bowlders and stones to the edge of the volcano.

From the margin of the lake to the other side of the mass of rocks was a hundred feet. This may be defined as a solid wall, shutting out the water from the burning mountain. The rocks rose to a height of a dozen rods or so, attaining which a spectator found himself half-way across the dividing ridge, where, viewed from the lake, his figure looked as if stamped in ink on the crimson background.

It was here that the lovers paused and viewed the striking picture spread out before their vision.

That which they saw might properly be considered the crater of the volcano. It was four or five acres in extent, irregular in contour, and so filled with gases and vapors that one could not see the bottom, while the jagged boundary on the farther side came out to view only at intervals, when the obstructing smoke was swept aside.

Spiral columns of black vapor twisted swiftly upward from the fiery depths, sometimes side by side, and sometimes they would unite and climb toward the opening above, like a couple of huge serpents struggling together. The air quivered and pulsated in certain portions, as if with fervid heat, and Ashman fancied once or twice that he caught glimpses of a vast mass of molten stuff, far down in the mountain, surging; seething and turning upon itself with terrific violence. But the glare was so dazzling that it was like staring at the sun, and he was compelled to withdraw his gaze.

The opening above, through which all this vapor and gas effected its escape into the clear atmosphere outside, was of irregular outline and no more than twenty feet across. It was at a great height above the spectators, and ought to have been visible many miles in every direction.

Now and then Ashman caught the odor of the sulphurous fumes rising from the naming depth, and he could not help reflecting that if the ascending vapors should swerve toward them only for a minute or two, they would be asphyxiated before they could get away; but he could not shrink, when his lovely companion stood so boldly by his side, unmoved by the impressive scene.

When he had become accustomed in a degree to the sight, the like of which he had never viewed before, he recalled that they could not occupy a more conspicuous position, in the event of being pursued by their enemies to the underground lake.

As we have explained, they were standing on the highest portion of the rocky wall, separating the burning mountain from the subterranean portion of the enchanted lake. In this situation, they were in sight from every portion of the shore; any one entering by the tunnel, as they had done, would descry them almost at once, because of the vivid background against which their figures were thrown.

This fact led Ashman to turn to his love and suggest that they should leave the spot. She nodded her head in acquiescence, and, still clasping hands, they began picking their way down among the bowlders to the spot where they had left their canoe a short time before.

CHAPTER XXXIII

THE PURSUERS

Haffgo, king of the Murhapas, intended to keep his promise to Ziffak, so far as permitting the explorers to remain in his village until the morrow, at which time he intended that the men should be allowed to go in safety.

But the barbarian was very similar to some of us whose resentment grows with reflection. When he recalled the admiring glances of the handsome young member of the company towards his beloved Ariel, his anger became intense, fanned by the strong suspicion that the princess herself felt some interest in the stranger.

At this critical time, Waggaman put in an appearance. The ruffian was shrewd enough to see his opportunity, and it took him but a few minutes to rouse him to the exploding point. He determined that every one of the whites should die, and he ordered the assault which has already been described.

As has been explained, the king kept within his home, while the attack was under way; but since he resided adjoining the structure which was assaulted, he was aware of every phase of the progress.

　　　　　　Edward S. Ellis

His rage has been hinted at because of the repulse of his warriors directly under his own eyes; but when he came to learn that the youth against whom his resentment burned so hotly was not within the building; that the two who had fought so bravely had escaped with their native helpers; that his own daughter the princess was absent; that she had been seen fleeing with the white youth in the direction of the enchanted lake:—when all this became known to the ruler, it may be said that his fury was such that no language could do it justice. It is not impossible that the despot felt thus himself, for, without pausing to give utterance to a few of his imaginings, he made instant preparations to follow the couple to the region which he never permitted a white man to look upon.

A native woman had seen the princess pass up the side of the river, followed a few minutes later by the young man. Her curiosity led her to watch them. She saw the two meet and stand for some time in loving converse. Then one of the white men stole behind them and was about to fire his dreadful weapon, when Ziffak hurled his terrible javelin which pinned him to the ground. Then the native woman hastened to the palace to tell the news, but she could not gain the chance for some time.

When the king turned upon his brother for an explanation of what he had done, Ziffak was prepared. It was the intention of Burkhardt to shoot not the white man but the princess herself, because she had refused his love. He heard Burkhardt mutter those words to himself and it was because of those words that Ziffak drove his javelin through his body.

King Haffgo looked sharply at his kinsman when he made this unblushing response, but his doubts if there were any quickly vanished, when he recalled the impetuosity with which he had attacked the defenders in the house and the vigor of his pursuit and his evident indignation and chagrin at the escape of the two white men. No, Ziffak might talk plainly with his royal brother, but when the time for action came he was a true Murhapa, who knew only his duty to his king.

Besides, the little flurry between the two had helped to clear away the fogs of misunderstanding as the lightning often purifies the murky atmosphere. The pursuit of the lovers was quickly organized, for they now occupied the thoughts of the king to the exclusion of everything else. Grimcke and Long could not be far off, and a vigorous hunt was likely to discover one or both of them, but the king gave orders that no attempt of the kind should be made. It was his intention to leave the village for an indefinite time, and he wished every one of his warriors to remain while he was absent. It cannot be said that he was afraid of such an insignificant force, but there was a strong vein of superstition in his nature, which caused a vague fear of the men that had escaped him with such wonderful cleverness. Individuals who could do *that* sort of thing, were capable of doing things still more marvellous, and to use homely language, King Haffgo was taking no chances.

The party in pursuit numbered just ten persona including the king, Ziffak, Waggaman, and the very pick of the tribe. They were all splendid fellows, fit to be the body-guard of a king, who, when he laid aside the robes of cumbrous dress he was accustomed to wear, and arrayed himself similarly to the warriors, proved himself no mean leader of such a party.

Any one looking upon the little company would have been most impressed by the fact that there were nine dusky barbarians, half naked and as black as Africans, under the guidance of a man as fair as any European; and yet, as the reader knows, the most prominent warrior of the party was

Edward S. Ellis

the brother of that king, dusky, tall and a giant in stature.

A tribe living in a country as well watered as the Matto Grosso, is sure to be well provided with the means of navigation, though the explorers, when they first reached the neighborhood of the rapids, deemed there was an unusual absence of such craft. A canoe, longer even than that used by our friends in ascending from the Amazon, was carried a short distance down the bank and launched in the Xingu. Five of the warriors seized their long paddles and swung them with the skill of veterans. They were accustomed to that kind of work, and sent the craft up the current with much greater speed than would have been suspected, even by those accustomed to see such work.

Two of the dusky occupants were furnished with bows and arrows, while Waggaman carried his rifle. Thus every species of weapon known to the Murhapas was in the boat.

King Haffgo sat at the stern, his brow dark and threatening, his arms folded and his lips set. His thoughts were too deep for utterance and no one ventured to disturb him. Though the pale countenance was outwardly calm, yet a volcano was raging in that breast, hot and furious enough to burst out and consume the barbarian.

Just in front of him, Ziffak was facing toward the prow, directing the actions of the crew, though for a time little of that was required of him. Waggaman was at the prow, silent, glum, scowling. He did not speak for a long while, but, now and then, glanced at Ziffak. When he did so, he was pretty sure to find the black eyes of the head chieftain fixed upon him.

The two thoroughly distrusted each other. Waggaman knew why that javelin had been driven through the body of his associate and, though the convict felt little sorrow for the loss of his companion, yet he hated the chieftain with a deadly hatred, well aware as he was that the feeling was thoroughly reciprocated by Ziffak.

Whether King Haffgo suspected the truth cannot be known, nor is it of importance to know. All the energy of his nature was concentrated in the emotion of fury against Fred Ashman, who had committed the unparalleled presumption of robbing him of his daughter; and even against that lovely maiden he was so incensed that he stood ready to bury his spear in her snowy bosom.

Though it may have seemed strange to Ashman that Ziffak had ordered him to make all haste to the enchanted lake, instead of starting on a direct flight through the woods, returning to the Xingu at a lower point, yet the sagacious chieftain had the best of reasons for his course, as will soon appear.

Had Ashman fled through the forest, the fact would have been discovered at daybreak, if not before, and such a vigorous pursuit would have been pressed as to render escape out of the question. There was a possibility of outwitting Haffgo by the flight to the lake, though it was remote enough to cause the giant warrior to shudder when he reflected upon it.

That which caused Ziffak regret was, that he had not paused long enough before parting from the couple, to arrange a better understanding with them. As it was, he was mostly in the dark concerning their movements, and greatly handicapped by the necessity of appearing to be the devoted ally of his royal brother.

Under the powerful propulsion of the five paddles, the long

Edward S. Ellis

narrow canoe sped swiftly up the Xingu, and, sooner than even Ziffak anticipated, it turned into the narrow stream leading to the enchanted lake. Along this it sped like a swallow until the huge rock with its sentinel came in sight.

It was here that King Haffgo, for the first time, showed some interest in his surroundings. He scanned the massive rock closely and manifestly was surprised that the guard did not rise to his feet and challenge them.

Observing that the figure remained motionless, he commanded the craft to approach the rock. This was silently done, the boat halting with the prow touching the mass of black stone.

Still the sentinel moved not, all unaware of his peril. One keen glance showed he was committing the unpardonable sin of sleeping at his post.

Rising quickly to his feet, the king stood upright for an instant, and then, with a furious exclamation, drove the javelin which he snatched from the hands of one of the warriors through the breast of the unfaithful servant, who uttered but a single groan as he perished by the hands of his master and sovereign.

Then Haffgo commanded one of his men to take his place. The fellow instantly sprang from the boat and took his station on the rock, as the successor of him who had died so ignominiously. Little fear of his falling asleep on his post.

A minute later the boat shot out upon the moonlit surface of the enchanted lake. There the occupants used their eyes for all they were worth, the craft making a partial circuit of the sheet of water. There was a possibility that the fugitives were there, though it was slight. Many places afforded a landing, where they might have found temporary shelter, but nothing was seen of the boat, and Haffgo ordered the oarsmen to pass through the tunnel leading to the underground lake.

This was speedily effected, and the large boat debouched into the wonderful body of water, so brilliantly illuminated by the glare from the burning mountain on the western side.

Instinctively every eye was cast in that direction, but nothing rewarded the scrutiny. Then the vision swept along the shores, every portion of which, as will be remembered, was in plain view.

Almost at the same moment; Ziffak uttered an excited exclamation, and pointed to the northern shore. As the gaze of every one was directed thither, they caught sight of the craft for which they were so eagerly hunting.

Edward S. Ellis

CHAPTER XXXIV

WATCHING AND WAITING

When Professor Ernest Grimcke realized that his desperate flight from the besieged building had been attended with complete success, and that he was standing among the dense shadows of the forest, with no enemy near, he devoutly uncovered his head, and, looking upward, uttered his fervent thanks to heaven for its amazing mercy.

"If ever a man was snatched from the jaws of death," he said, "I am that man."

"And I am another," added Jared Long, who approached in the gloom. "It seems to me like a veritable miracle."

The New Englander explained that, after his furious dash for shelter from the building, he did not believe his chances were any better than those of the man he left behind him. He started, with the intention of making his way by a circuitous course to the river, but had not gone far when he was struck by the baseness of his desertion of his friend. He, therefore, turned about with the resolve to try to do something for him, but had no more than caught sight of the structure again when he descried the Professor coming like a whirlwind for the trees.

Long moved to the point at which he saw he was aiming, and held his Winchester ready to open on any pursuers that might try to follow him. He would have picked off a dozen or so, for he was cool and collected, and fully determined to stand by his friend to the death.

Fortunately, however, for all parties concerned, none of the Murhapas pursued the Professor, though, as has been told, a number under the leadership of Ziffak dashed off in another direction, without endangering the fugitives in the least.

It was a marvellous deliverance, indeed, for our friends, and they understood the part the giant head chieftain had taken in extricating them from the peril. Their hearts glowed with gratitude to the savage, whose friendship for them they could not understand, but who had proven it in such a striking manner.

But it could not be said that they were yet free from danger; and there was much to do before they could breathe freely.

It needed but a brief consultation to agree that after what had taken place, it was the height of madness to attempt to push on to the enchanted lake and burning mountain. King Haffgo was so roused that there was not the slightest chance of escape. The only earthly probability of accomplishing anything in that direction, was by bringing a force strong enough to sweep the warlike Murhapas from their path.

Thankful would the little party of explorers be if they were permitted to get out of the Matto Grosso with their lives.

They waited in the margin of the wood until the return of Ziffak and his baffled company. It was easy to understand the clever trick played by the chieftain upon his followers, and Grimcke and Long were convinced that no further

Edward S. Ellis

attempt, at least for a time, would be made to capture them.

But being free to attend to their own safety, their thoughts naturally turned to the missing members of the company, especially to Ashman, who unquestionably was involved in the most imminent peril.

It was clear that his two friends could do nothing in his behalf. They did not know where to look for him, and such an attempt was sure to be followed by disastrous conesquences to themselves.

It was a singular conclusion to which Grimcke and Long arrived and yet perhaps it was natural. They believed that Ashman had escaped before they did themselves, and that he was probably waiting at some point down the Xingu for them. They decided to pass in the same direction and strive to open communication with him.

How little did they suspect that though he was for the time out of the power of his enemies, yet the Princess Ariel was his companion, and that instead of seeking to flee from the dangerous country, he had actually penetrated farther into it.

After carefully reconnoitering their surroundings, therefore, the Professor and Long approached the Xingu at a point a third of a mile below the Murhapa village. Everything seemed to be quiet and motionless around them, with the exception of the river, yet they were given precious little time for wonderment or speculation.

The first amazing sight on which their eyes rested was their own large canoe drifting down stream. They stood a moment, not knowing what to make of it, but speedily reached the right conclusion: Ziffak had set it free for their special benefit.

It was floating sideways near the middle of the Xingu, and showed there was no one on board.

It was too invaluable to be allowed to get away from them, or to run the risk of a passage through the rapids below. Long decided to swim out to it, but, before he could enter the water, the Professor showed him that some one had anticipated them. A short distance up the bank, a native was in the act of entering the Xingu, while his companion stood on the bank, evidently about to follow him.

The clear moonlight enabled the explorers to identify them as Bippo and Pedros, the former being the one already in the water.

"Let them go," whispered the Professor, "they may as well do it for us."

Pedros was but a few strokes behind his friend, and the two were seen to clamber over the side of the craft at the moment it came opposite where the delighted white men were standing.

At this juncture, the Professor called to them in a guarded voice. Their expressions of amazement were ludicrous, and it was only after they had stared for several minutes and the call was repeated that they comprehended that their friends were near.

Then the two showed their extravagant delight by leaping up and down like a couple of children, and uttering cries that, to say the least, were imprudent.

The Professor sternly ordered them to hold their peace and paddle the boat to shore. They set to work with a will and brought the craft to land, only a short distance below, where the white men had reached the river. Instantly, they stepped on board, and with the exception of the single absent member, our friends stood in the same situation as a short time before.

It was Jared Long that in his flight from the beleaguered building took the extra Winchester with him, so that the little party could not have been better armed. Luckily, too, there was an abundant supply of ammunition on board, so that the old feeling of confidence came back to the party when they once more felt they were masters of the boat and all it contained.

Their desire now was to increase the distance between themselves and the Murhapa village, from which all had had such a narrow escape. When Bippo timidly asked his masters whether they meant to return or attempt to go any farther up the Xingu, they were assured that no such thought was in the mind of either of the explorers. They would only be thankful if they could get back to the Amazon without ever meeting another Murhapa.

This was enough for the natives, who were willing to jump overboard and tow the boat faster than it was already going. That, however, was unnecessary, and they were told that they had only to obey orders as cheerfully as they had done from the beginning and that undoubtedly everything would come out well.

It was past midnight, when the roaring just below, which was increasing every minute, warned them they were approaching the dangerous rapids. Possibly the craft might have passed safely through but it would have been imprudent to make the attempt for which no necessity existed.

Accordingly, the boat was once more run ashore and drawn

against the bank, with the view of raising it upon their shoulders to be transported to the calmer waters below.

The four men were in the very act of lifting the craft, when to their terror, fully a score of Aryks suddenly emerged from the wood and surrounded them. All were armed with the frightful javelins, a prick from one of which was enough to cause almost instant death.

The whites could not have been caught at greater disadvantage, and Bippo and Pedros were so overcome that they were unable to move. Long was on the point of opening a fusillade, when Professor Grimcke was struck by the fact that no one of the Aryks offered to harm them. They chattered like a lot of magpies, and gathering round them made a movement as if to take possession of their boat.

The New Englander would have showed fight, had not his companion said in a low tone:

"They are friendly! They mean to do us no harm!"

Such was the astounding truth, and it was easily explained. Ziffak on his way up the Xingu with his new friends had warned the Aryks that they must do the whites no harm: they were on their way at that time to the Murhapa village as friends, and the head chieftain told his allies that any further hostility would be visited with the punishment of death.

The Aryks were not likely to forget such a notice. They had seen the boat approaching; and, being totally unsuspicious of what had occurred during the earlier part of the evening, were anxious to manifest their good will by carrying the canoe around the rapids.

Jared Long could hardly credit the truth, and held himself

Edward S. Ellis

ready for a desperate fight; but, when the boat was lifted upon the shoulders of a half dozen stalwart warriors who started down the shore with it, he smiled grimly and admitted that the Professor was right.

The load was quite burdensome, but the carriers stepped off, highly pleased with the privilege, while the rest of their party straggled after them, the whites and their servants bringing up the rear.

Bippo and Pedros were not quite able to comprehend the extraordinary condition of affairs, and kept close to the heels of their masters like a couple of frightened dogs.

At the base of the rapids, the Aryks set down the boat, with great care, saluted in their rude way, and turning about, disappeared in the forest from which they had emerged.

"*If they only knew*," said Long when they were drifting down stream once more.

"But they *don't*," replied the Professor, "and yet they will learn the truth before long."

The boat was allowed to drift a half mile further, when, convinced they had gone far enough, they ran into land, disembarked and carried it in among the trees, where it was out of the sight of any one passing up or down the Xingu. Then they prepared to await the coming of Fred Ashman, doubtful, however, whether he ever would come.

CHAPTER XXXV

THE CAVERN OF DIAMONDS

Fred Ashman was greatly relieved when he had assisted Ariel down from the high, rocky wall, and they had picked their way to the spot where the little canoe had been left but a short time before.

He had felt a singular misgiving from the first about the boat, fearful that in this region of enchantment, as it seemed to him, something would cause it to disappear, and he and his lovely companion be left in a most exposed and dangerous situation.

But it was found just where it had been left, and helping her in it, he shoved it clear and then looked to her for directions as to what was to be the next step.

The maiden now made a singular statement. She said that some weeks before, she had visited this place with no companion but her father. They landed at a point which she indicated, and he ordered her to stay on the shore until his return. He was gone so long, however, that she undertook a little exploration on her own account, and made a discovery which she now hoped to turn to account.

Edward S. Ellis

The canoe touched at the spot she pointed out, and they stepped ashore. She said that her parent strolled off to the left, toward a passage which she showed, and which she had entered with him several times before, but from which he seemed desirous to exclude her on the occasion named.

It was while he was absent at that time, that Ariel walked some distance to the right. She clambered up the rocks a little way to a clump of bushes. She was examining a species of crimson berry, growing upon them, when she observed a passage, which she followed far enough to find that it led into a large cavern, whose full extent she did not attempt to learn. She withdrew, and, fearful of offending the king, told him nothing about it when he returned and found her with the boat.

Ariel was confident that neither her parent nor any of her people knew of her discovery, and she now proposed to Ashman that they should enter the strange cavern, and remain until the present danger was over. She believed that if her friends or enemies, as they might be considered, did not discover them soon, they would conclude that they had voluntarily met death together, and would give up the hunt.

Ashman was struck with the sagacity of the lady, and eagerly agreed to her suggestion. It would never do to leave the canoe as a tell-tale, and he gave it a shove which carried it far out on the lake. Discovered in that situation, no one could tell what point on the shore it had touched, and, being adrift, near the middle of the lake, it would suggest the theory of suicide, which they were anxious to impress upon their pursuers.

Carefully picking their way through the mass of brush and undergrowth which showed remarkable vigor, considering that the revivifying sunlight never touched it, Ashman readily found the opening described by his companion.

It was just broad enough to allow the passage of their bodies, its height being such that they could move by stooping slightly. Holding his Winchester in hand, he led the way with Ariel pressing him close.

The same fact was noticeable that struck him when paddling through the tunnel connecting the outer and the underground lake. The light increased as they progressed until everything was seen with a distinctness hardly less than that shown in the water they had just left behind them.

Suddenly Ashman paused with an expression of amazement. He had entered a cavern so striking in appearance that it almost took away his wreath.

It was several acres in extent, with an arching, dome-like roof rising fully two hundred feet above their heads. Stalactites and stalagmites dozens of feet in length were visible hanging from the roof and obtruding from the floor, the latter being broken by chasms and ravines, many of which seemed to have a depth that was fathomless.

No water was visible, but the proximity of the lake rendered it likely that some of the abysses were filled at the bottom with the element. It looked impossible for the lovers to advance beyond the entrance, and yet while Ashman was standing motionless he observed that a ledge put out on their right, along which they could make their way indefinitely, its course being hidden by scores of intervening obstacles.

It looked like a scene of enchantment indeed, the wonderful cavern illumined by the flood of crimson light, which was on every hand, while the radiating point was invisible.

Edward S. Ellis

Ariel stood silent and waited for her companion to recover from his astonishment. She had viewed all this before and had witnessed so many similar scenes that they produced less effect upon her imagination than upon his.

By and by he looked around, and she smilingly nodded her head. He began picking his way along the ledge, carefully feeling his way, for a misstep or a treacherous support was liable to precipitate him to the fathomless depths below with the inevitable certainty of instant death.

It was while the young American was working forward in this guarded manner, that he particularly noticed that the roof overhead, and all parts of the walls were dotted with what seemed points of living fire. While some were small, others were larger and gave out a light that was dazzling to the point of blindness.

He supposed they were composed of a species of quartz or mineral, but observing one of them within reach at his side, he reached upward with his knife and extracted it from the shale in which it was imbedded.

Taking it in his hand he turned it over several times with increasing curiosity. It appeared to be a rough pebble, from which he brushed away a portion of the dirt, so as to permit it to shine with a splendor that would have been tenfold greater in the full light of the sun.

"Don't you know what it is?" asked Ariel with another smile at his perplexed expression.

"I do not; can you tell me?"

"It is a diamond!"

"And," he asked, with a sweep of his arm, "are all those diamonds?"

"They are."

"Great heavens!" gasped the astounded Ashman; "we have entered a cavern of diamonds."

"There can be no doubt of that," she calmly replied; "there are plenty of them among the rocks along other portions of the lake, for that is where the king has obtained them for years. There is gold there too. You know now the reason why he guards the approaches of the lake so jealously. I have seen our men digging for diamonds and they looked just like what these seem around us."

Ashman had paused again and his eyes roved around the magnificent scene, whose splendors were enough to turn the head of Solomon himself. Thousands of the points were gleaming from all portions of the roof, walls, and even on the ledge along which they were walking. There was enough wealth within his gaze to pay the national debt of his country and to effect a revolution in any nation.

"I would be a fool," he reflected, "not to gather some of these while the chance is mine, even though I may never live to carry them away."

CHAPTER XXXVI

PURSUERS AND PURSUED

It may be doubted whether the most cool-headed of men could find himself in such a situation as that of Fred Ashman, without being overwhelmed by the bewildering wealth surrounding him. He forgot for the time that the lives of himself and lovely companion were at stake, and that, despite her assurance that they were the first persons who had ever entered the wonderful cavern of diamonds, its existence might be known or discovered by their vengeful pursuers.

With the aid of his hunting knife, he set himself to work picking out the precious gems that were within his reach at all times.

Now and then, when some one of unusual size fell into his palm he uttered an exclamation of delight, and turned and held it up for Ariel to admire. She smiled at his pleasure, and showed her sympathy by assisting in the excavation of the marvellous pebbles.

As they toiled, they advanced, sometimes a step at a time, and then for several paces. Conscious that he could carry away only an infinitely small portion of the riches, Ashman found himself in the unparalleled situation of casting aside the smaller gems and taking only those that were large and of the first water.

Who before was compelled to fling away diamonds worth hundreds of dollars apiece, simply because they were of too insignificant value to be carried with him? Ariel, who was a much better expert than he, carefully selected the choicest until she was burdened with all she could conveniently carry. He filled his pockets and thrust others into every receptacle at command. The partially emptied cartridge-belt was made to do duty as a casket, and it is safe to say that no similar contrivance was ever laden with a tithe of the riches that particular one held.

"Ah," reflected the young man again and again, "if only the Professor and Long were here to help me!"

But there came the time, all too soon, when he was forced to admit that it was useless to attempt to carry more. He had the wealth of a prince about his person, and yet the storehouse showed no diminution of its boundless supply, which was enough to burden a regiment of soldiers.

Gold, the most precious of all metals, for which men delve and starve and toil and die, still lies hidden in immeasurable masses, in unsuspected places, screened perhaps by a thin sheeting of earth, over which thousands have tramped, never dreaming of the boundless riches just beneath their feet. And rubies and diamonds strew the bottom of the ocean or scintillate within caverns and caves, as they have shone and gleamed through ages, still waiting for the fortunate miner or explorer to bring them to light and the gaze of an admiring world.

"If I ever live to get away from this spot," added Ashman,

Edward S. Ellis

when he ceased his wonderful garnering, "I will bring a force here; I can afford to make it irresistible by King Haffgo, for every one of the men can take away a fortune and leave more than enough for these barbarians."

"I can take no more," he said, turning his flushed face upon the radiant countenance just behind him; "King Haffgo will never miss these, but when I carry you to my distant home, Ariel, where I shall cherish and love you forever, these diamonds will bring us such wealth that we shall never know the meaning of want; every luxury that affection can dream of, or heart can crave, shall be yours."

"The greatest luxury my heart yearns for," said she softly, "is *your* love."

"And that you have now," he replied catching her in his arms and straining her to his heart.

"I am sure of it," replied the happy maiden, resisting no longer the ardent embrace of him whose affection seemed to grow with every passing hour.

"All that I pray heaven to grant is the opportunity to prove to you that you are not mistaken. I do not want to leave here or ever see my home again unless you are with me. I shall live or die with you, for death with you is preferable to life without you, my cherished, my own Ariel."

The radiant countenance was illumined by a light such as only the divine passion can impart. She did not speak, for there are some emotions of the soul beyond the power of language.

The hunt for the diamonds had taken the lovers to a point almost opposite the entrance. They observed what they had not noticed during their absorbing work,—the ledge along which they advanced, steadily ascended until it carried them to a point half-way to the top of the mighty dome. Standing there, they could look back on the awful chasms spread below their feet, the crimsoned walls, sparkling and scintillating with innumerable gems, with the craggy roof seemingly almost within their reach.

Looking over the wild, dazzling, unapproachable scene, the American was considering the practical question of what was next to be done, when Ariel at his side abruptly seized his arm with an intensity which startled and caused him to ask,

"What has frightened you, dearest?"

With a gasp, she pointed to the other side of the cavern, where they had entered this region of enchantment and wonders.

A procession of figures was moving along the ledge, over which they had just made their way. The intervening objects shut them partly out of sight, but the heads and shoulders of several were always in view and they were moving with the utmost haste possible.

The foremost figure was a white man; the next was a dusky giant, and the third was of fair complexion, while all the others were of the hue of native Africans.

There could be no mistaking the identity of the leaders: the foremost was Waggaman, the second, Ziffak, and the third, King Haffgo. Those who followed were the pick of the Murhapa warriors.

It mattered not whether Ariel was right in her belief that the existence of the cavern of diamonds was unknown to every one else, or that some fateful good fortune had directed the party to the entrance. It was enough that they had found it, and were now pressing forward along the very ridge on which they had halted, and stood gazing back in amazement and horror, unable for the moment to divine what could be done to help themselves.

But Ashman needed but a few seconds to decide his course. He held his Winchester and revolver and was ready to die in the defence of the idol of his heart.

"Have courage," he said; "all is not yet lost."

The ledge on which they stood was so narrow that there was no room for two to walk beside each other. Lifting the gentle form in one arm, he swung her over the abyss at his feet and placed her on the ledge in front of him.

The danger was at the rear, and that was the place for him.

"Now advance," he added; "we may find a better spot than this for defence."

He feared that his pursuers might divide, and some of them start around the other way, so as to come upon him from the opposite side. If that were done, he would be caught between two fires; and, since one of the party possessed a gun, the advantage would be preponderatingly against him.

There was subject, too, for perplexing thought in the situation. He had no wish to shoot King Haffgo, and would not do it if any possible way of avoiding it should present itself. He determined that he should be spared until the last one, when he could probably be handled, without resorting to the last extremity.

Then, too, he felt no doubt about the presence of the giant Ziffak. He was the friend of himself and Ariel, though for politic reasons he had assumed the guise of an enemy. His situation was a most delicate one, and, even in his bewilderment and anxiety, Ashman could not help wondering how he would conduct himself in the crisis at hand.

Inasmuch as the American was resolved to avoid injuring the dusky Hercules, it will be observed that there were two of the company of pursuers whom he was much more anxious to spare than he was to inflict harm upon the rest.

He was hopeful for a moment that he and his companion had not been detected, but a resounding shout echoed through the cavern of diamonds—a shout of such amazing power that he knew it had come from the throat of Ziffak himself, who, as if to make sure his meaning was not misunderstood, brandished his mighty javelin over his prodigious head and shoulders, as he almost pushed his leader from the path in front of him.

CHAPTER XXXVII

AT BAY

Ariel flitted so rapidly along the ledge that her lover felt obliged to ask her to desist, as he found it difficult to keep pace with her.

The narrow path ascended more rapidly than before, and he saw they were steadily climbing toward the top of the roof. The shelly support to their feet, too, became less substantial, crumbling and giving way at a rate that threatened the most serious consequences.

He again cautioned the maiden, who seemed to dart over the rocky ground with the graceful ease of a bird, and without producing any more effect, with her dainty sandals.

Suddenly she paused. She had reached the margin or break in the ledge. A chasm, whose black depths the eye could not fathom, yawned between her and the support on the opposite side.

"We will make our stand here," said he; "keep behind me—"

He checked himself in astonishment; for, at that moment, she bounded as lightly across as a fawn. He never would have permitted it had he dreamed of her intention; but it was done.

He could only follow, and, gathering his muscles, he ran rapidly the slight distance and bounded from the support.

It was a tremendous leap, and, for one instant, he believed he would fail; but he cleared the chasm of breathless darkness and landed on the edge, where, for a single second, he tottered between life and death.

But, at the critical instant, a tiny hand was outstretched, and, seizing one of the fluttering arms, his poise was restored, and he stood firmly by her side.

Even then, as he stepped forward, the ground crumbled and gave way for fully two feet, the debris rattling down the abyss as long as the ear could detect the sound, growing fainter and fainter as it hastened toward the far-away bottom.

"There is no one in that party except Ziffak who can leap it now," said Ashman, gazing with a shudder behind him.

By this time the pursuers were close at hand and gaining fast.

The ledge led straight away and upward for a hundred feet, when it terminated at a point in the dome as high as the middle portion. There the rocks were piled in irregular masses, and, knowing they could go no further, Ashman resolved that the last stand should be made there.

As he hurried onward, another shout fell upon his ear. It was a different voice, and he recognized it as Waggaman's, who was leading the advance.

The fugitive glanced backward, while toiling up the slope, and saw that the white man in his eagerness was fully a rod

Edward S. Ellis

ahead of the herculean Ziffak, while the rest were stringing along behind him.

He might have wondered how the chieftain contrived to lose so much ground had he not seen him clambering to his feet. It followed that he must have fallen in his hurry to get forward.

"We have them!" shouted the exultant convict; "there is no escape; they are cornered!"

The words were yet ringing in his mouth, when he came to a stop.

He had reached the edge of the abyss and might well pause before trying to leap across.

The fierce king called to him to make the jump. It had been done not only by the man, but by the girl who preceded him; why should he hesitate?

Spurred by the taunt, the white man withdrew a few paces, and, like Ashman, ran swiftly, the next instant his body rising in air, as he made the fatal effort.

The American stood coolly watching the result. If the miscreant succeeded, where it looked impossible, he meant to shoot him. Thus the prospect before the convict could not have been worse.

It was a tremendous leap indeed, and the fellow struck the opposite ledge with his chest, his feet dropping below.

In his furious efforts to save himself, he let go of his weapon, which went ringing down the chasm, and seized the ledge with both hands.

Even then, had the ground been firm, he might have succeeded, but it gave way like rotten ice, and, with a shriek of agony, he vanished forever from the sight of men.

The frightful occurrence brought the pursuers to a halt and gave the fugitives a minute or two in which to prepare for the end.

Ariel, by command of her lover, placed herself behind the rocks and bowlders, where she was secure against any of the missiles, that were sure to be soon flying through the air. Ashman also placed himself so that all of his body was hidden, except his head and shoulders, but his Winchester was thrust out, ready for instant use. He was resolved that no one of the party should leap that chasm and live after reaching the other side.

There were two exceptions, be it remembered, to this resolution.

Ziffak, being next to Waggaman, approached the chasm, where he also stopped and peered into the impenetrable depth, his dusky face showing a horrified expression at the awful fate that had befallen the foremost of the little party.

Ashman, who was closely watching the chieftain with a natural wonder us to how he would conduct himself (for he did not waver in his faith that the giant was still loyal to him), saw him suddenly raise his eyes and gaze at the opposite ledge, which was fully two feet above that upon which he was standing.

Haffgo was immediately behind him, and peering under his arms at the opening. There being no room for the two to stand beside each other, this was the nearest position he could secure.

Edward S. Ellis

Beyond him the other figures could be partly discerned, all standing motionless until some way should present itself for their advance.

Ashman observed the chieftain, as his eyes followed the ledge until they rested upon him, crouching behind one of the bowlders with his rifle leveled at the war party.

The two looked into each other's eyes for a single instant, when Ziffak, knowing he could not be seen by any of those behind, contracted his brows and moved his lips.

He did not speak, for that would have "given the whole thing away," but his dusky mouth was contorted with such vigorous care that the words were understood, as readily as if shouted aloud.

They formed the single sentence,

"*I am your friend!*"

No need of saying that, for, as we have stated, Fred Ashman had never doubted it.

Haffgo now began urging his brother to make the leap, which had proven the death of Waggaman, saying, with reason, that the strength and activity of the head chieftain of the Murhapas were sure to carry him over where no one else could succeed.

The two talked in their native tongue, but their meaning was so clear that the American needed no one to interpret the words.

Ziffak replied that he would gladly do so, but for the treacherous character of the other side of the ledge. He showed that considerable had fallen away, and intimated that the fugitives had loosened it for the purpose of entrapping all the party just as Waggaman had been entrapped.

Then the king took another look at the chasm. It so happened that while he was doing this, a large slice of the ledge sloughed off and went down the abyss, after the miserable wretch who must have been lying at that moment a shapeless mass far down the fearful gorge.

Haffgo could not gainsay such testimony, and, for the first time, his face showed an expression of disappointment. It was not the look of a baffled man, but of one forced to see a sweet pleasure deferred.

He had only to peer up the ledge, as it led toward the roof, to realize that the fugitives were as safely caged as if bound and secured in his own home.

They had penetrated as far as possible in the cavern of diamonds. If the pursuers could not reach them, neither could they return over the chasm by which they had attained the spot where they still defied him.

The most athletic man living could not leap across that chasm, nor could it be passed until it was bridged artificially, and that could only be accomplished from below, where the pursuers were glaring across. They might erect a structure, if, the king so willed, which would open a way of advance; but he was in no mood to care for or think of anything of the kind.

Haffgo now talked earnestly for a few minutes to his head chieftain. The latter listened respectfully, nodding his head several times in acquiescence. Then he suddenly looked up the ledge again, steadied himself for an instant, and hurled

Edward S. Ellis

his javelin with terrific force at the head of Ashman.

It was done with such incredible deftness that the American had no time in which to dodge the fearful missile. Had it been accurately aimed, it would have been driven straight through his skull!

But it missed by a hair's breadth, shooting up to the roof, where it struck the rock with such violence that the head was shattered and the remaining portion fell uselessly down among the rocks.

It was a close call, but Ashman was not frightened; he knew why it missed him.

He now sighted along the barrel, as if he meant to shoot the chieftain, who instantly ducked his head, and began crowding backward. It was the first time King Haffgo had been placed in such a grave situation, and he was panic-stricken. He turned so suddenly and began crowding to the rear so hard, that he came within a hair of precipitating himself and those immediately behind him from the ledge.

But Ashman did not pull trigger. He could not do so without endangering the lives of Ziffak and the king, and as yet the other warriors had made no demonstration against him.

But, seeing that the white man did not fire, Ziffak seemed to gather courage and straightened up again. The king passed his own javelin to him, and he glared up the ledge as if looking for another favorable chance to launch, it with greater effect than before.

Ashman, who was narrowly watching every movement of his enemies, now observed that the warrior directly behind the king, carried a bow and arrow, and he was in the act of fitting a missile to the string, with the evident intention of trying his hand at the business in which the head chieftain had failed only a minute before.

Edward S. Ellis

CHAPTER XXXVIII

THE POISONED ARROW

Such being the case, Ashman concluded that the time had arrived when he should also take a hand.

Ziffak and King Haffgo placed their backs against the face of the rocks, along which the ledge ran, so as to open a clear course for the archer. The latter fitted his arrow with great care and then straightening up drew back the string and slowly levelled, the missile at the head and breast of the American.

"Does that fool imagine I am going to keep still and let him practice on me?" the latter asked himself, an instant before discharging his rifle, whose bullet went straight through the dusky miscreant and sent him toppling off the side of the ledge as dead as dead could be.

Not only that, but the ball wounded the warrior directly behind him, causing him to utter a howl which rang with piercing force from side to side of the cavern of diamonds.

This prompt act caused something like a panic, Ziffak seemed the most terrified of any. Facing about, he flung his arms aloft and shouted to the rest to hurry away before the white man killed them all.

They lost no time in obeying, and it was noticeable that King Haffgo, being well at the rear, added his frenzied commands for his warriors to lose no time in leaving the fatal spot.

Ashman could have sent a succession of shots along the ridge, as the party scrambled away, which would have toppled the dusky barbarians off like so many ten-pins; but he had no desire to inflict needless slaughter, and, in answer to the appeal of the shrinking Ariel, he had promised her that, so far as he was concerned, her parent should receive no harm.

He therefore contented himself with watching them, until a bend in the ledge hid them from sight, with the exception of their heads, and they, too, soon disappeared; because the frightened warriors, glancing back, and seeing their peril, crouched low to escape the bullets which they seemed to expect would come whistling about their crowns.

As long as the natives kept at such a distance, they could do no harm to the defenders; for they were too far off to make use of their javelins, and the single archer left was not likely to attempt to bring his weapon into play.

Naturally, Ashman and Ariel, finding they were left to themselves for a time, fell to speculating upon what was likely to be the next move of their enemies. He believed they would make an attempt to bridge the chasm separating them, a task which, as will be seen, was comparatively easy of accomplishment.

But should such a structure be laid, it must be so strait that only one could pass at a time, and the American could pick them off as often as they presented themselves. There were now no firearms at the command of the Murhapas, unless some one recovered the weapon of Burkhardt, and even then, Ashman would feel little fear of harm from the savages.

Ariel thought her parent and his little company would simply keep guard at the entrance of the cavern, in order to intercept them, if they discovered some way of re-crossing the chasm and attempted to leave.

But both were wrong.

The young man was resolved that no march should be stolen upon him. It was impossible for the Murhapas to pass far enough around to leave the place, without being seen, provided he kept unremitting watch, which he felt competent to do for a number of hours to come.

If the siege was prolonged, he could take turns with Ariel, whose bright eyes were quicker of perception than his.

In the cavern of diamonds, there was no means of telling when it was day or night on the earth outside. Lit by the eternal fires of the volcano, it was always day; but he carried a watch, which told him that the night was far advanced, and that the bright sun would soon shine upon mountain, forest, and river again, though his heart sank at the faint prospect of it ever being his privilege to greet the orb again.

The incidents of the next hour mystified both Ashman and Ariel.

The first movement which attracted their notice, was Ziffak, who, rising to the upright posture, so that his immense shoulders were in plain sight, was seen picking his way along the ledge, until he reached the opening on the other side. Through this he passed and was seen no more.

It was useless to speculate as to the meaning of this proceeding, which could not be explained until made clear by occurrences themselves. It was safe to assume, however, that it was ostensibly in the interests of King Haffgo, and therefore against those of the fugitive lovers.

Probably a half-hour after the disappearance of the chieftain, two of the party were seen stealing along the ledge in the direction of the entrance to the cavern. These, however, were of such slight stature, when compared with Ziffak, and they made such efforts to conceal their movements, that it was hard to follow or identify them. Ashman thought that Haffgo was one of the number, but he could not make certain, and, since Ariel did not catch as favoring a glimpse as he, she could give no help in solving the question.

The best solution of the singular acts was that while the Murhapas seemed to try to hide themselves from the lovers, they still took pains to allow enough to be disclosed to reveal the movements, which they wished the couple to observe.

And here again, both Ashman and Ariel were in error.

Strange that a possibility which had once been thought of by the two did not occur again to them.

King Haffgo, despite his confidence in Ziffak, began to feel some distrust of him. His refusal to attempt the leap of the chasm, and his former friendship for the explorers, might have been reasonably explained, but his failure to drive his javelin through the white man, who was so near and who never stirred from his position, could not be an accident. He knew the marvellous skill of the head chieftain, who could have had but one cause for missing Ashman: that was an intentional deviation of his weapon, which, slight though it was, proved as effective as if hurled in the opposite direction.

And yet, shrewd as was Ziffak; he really believed he had deceived his royal brother. No suspicion of the distrust in the mind of the king came to the chieftain, when he was directed to return to the village and bring ten more warriors with him.

But this errand secured the absence of Ziffak for a couple of hours at least, and that was the sole purpose of Haffgo in sending him out of the cavern of diamonds.

When the chieftain was gone, the archer was directed to ascertain how far he could steal around the cavern, by taking the opposite course. Haffgo followed, directing the others to stay where they were until further orders were given them.

The archer set out at once, ahead of the king, both doing their best to avoid detection.

Fortune favored them in an unexpected manner. The ledge was found easier of travel than they expected, and, by using great care, they worked their way to a point less than two hundred feet from where the fugitives were standing on guard. They had traversed the whole distance, too, without detection.

When King Haffgo peered carefully over the shoulders of the crouching bowman, he saw the couple standing with their backs toward him, as they faced the chasm which had been found impassable for the Murhapas.

The slumbering anger in the parent's breast was kindled to a white heat, when he observed the white man holding the hand of his daughter, and he saw him lean over and touch his lips to hers. He whispered to the warrior to lose no time.

The latter quickly examined his arrows, and picked out the one which not only seemed the best, but was most plentifully provided with the deadly poison. This was speedily fitted to the string, and he deliberately took aim, his nerves like steel, for the king had whispered to him that he must not fail.

At the instant the string twanged, something caused Ariel to look behind them.

She uttered a faint scream as she caught sight of the two crouching figures. She descried a flitting shadow which she knew was the approaching missile on its deadly mission.

Knowing that it was aimed at her lover, she threw both her arms around his neck and interposed her body to protect him while he stood bewildered, not comprehending what it all meant.

Her figure was too slight to serve the purpose of a shield. The poisoned arrow whizzed straight at the breast of Ashman, who had turned about, but instead of entering his body, the point, surcharged with venom, was imbedded in the snowy arm of Ariel herself!

CHAPTER XXXIX

CONCLUSION

The horrified Fred Ashman saw that the poisoned arrow, aimed at his own heart had buried itself in the fair arm of Ariel, as she clasped him about the neck anxious to shield him from harm at the expense of her own life.

She had saved him, but at what a fearful cost! The agonized lover realized it all, as he tenderly placed her on the rock beside which they were standing. Then, like the man who, knowing he has been fatally struck by the rattlesnake or cobra, turns to stamp the life out of the reptile, before looking after his own wound, he faced about and brought his rifle to his shoulder. The dusky miscreant cowered low, but he could not save himself, for the bullet which left the Winchester, entering at the skull, ranged through the length of his body, and he rolled off the ledge like a rotten log and went down the yawning abyss that afforded a fit sepulture for such as he.

King Haffgo was standing erect, as if defying the white man to fire at him. He had seen the result of the shot and he did not regret it.

"Die the death you deserve!" he called out in English; "for

you are not the daughter of Haffgo!"

Then he turned about and moved along the ledge, while Ashman stood for an instant, with weapon levelled, feeling that the awful occurrence had absolved him from the pledge made a short time before.

He was aiming, when a faint voice at his side said:

"No, hurt him not; *I shall get well*!"

Letting the rifle fall from his grasp, he wheeled around as if he had been shot himself.

What did he see?

The brave Ariel had drawn the arrow from her arm, and was sitting erect. In her right hand, was a small earthen bottle such as was in common use among the Murhapas.

"Great heaven! what does this mean?" demanded her lover, uncertain whether he was awake or dreaming.

She smiled faintly, and said:

"I feel a little faint, but the danger is past."

"But,—but,"—he added, "the arrow was poisoned!"

"Yes, but the poison has a remedy; it is in *that*," she added, holding up the bottle; "my parent always carried it; I brought it with me when I left home."

The overjoyed lover could not repress a shout of joy,—a shout which penetrated every portion of the cavern of diamonds, but whose meaning, fortunately for the couple, was not understood by the ears on which it fell.

He knelt beside her, so that the bowlders shut both from the view of any prowlers who might seek to reach them. He kissed the happy face again and again; he called her the sweetest names that ever mortal uttered, and he assured her that they should both live and be happy forever.

In his overflowing bliss, he could not realize that they were still walled in on every hand. All that he could know and feel, was, that she was spared from a dreadful death,—that she had interposed her own precious body to protect him from harm.

Enwrapped in his arms, she was obliged to confess that the bringing of the potent remedy was an inspiration, when she stole out of her father's house, for she never dreamed of the use to which it would be put.

She had forgotten all about it, until the sharp twinge in her arm apprised her that she was struck by the fearful missile. Then, as she was about to swoon, she recalled that she carried the remedy in her bosom.

Drawing it quickly forth, while her lover's face was turned away, she drank the whole contents, which were sufficient to save the lives of three or four persons. Not a drop, however, was left; and she remarked in her own peculiar manner, that they must be careful not to be struck by any more such missiles, since the remedy was gone, and it would be hard to secure more.

With a full realization of the remarkable deliverance of his beloved, Ashman was roused to a stronger resolution than before of making a desperate effort to extricate themselves from their perilous situation, which looked indeed as if without hope.

Rising to his feet, but screening his body as he could, he carefully peered around the cavern of diamonds. He cautioned Ariel to keep out of sight, for, if it should become know that her life was saved, her father and his warriors would doubtless make another attempt to reach them.

Looking in the direction of the opening on the other side, he saw Haffgo pass out, followed the next minute or two by the rest of the Murhapas. To Ashman this was proof that the party had decided to withdraw from the cavern, but would keep watch of the egress to make sure that the white man did not get away by some freak of fortune.

Since they were sure he was caught in a trap from which there was no escape, he had his choice of remaining and starving to death, of coming forth and giving himself up, or of ending it all by precipitating himself down the rocks.

A terrible punishment indeed for the white man that had dared to defy the king of the Murhapas, and had been the cause of the death of the beloved princess!

Ashman was still studying the insoluble problem, when a strange impulse led him to look aloft. It will be remembered that he was near the roof of the cavern, among a mass of bowlders and rocks which touched the dome.

Several times it had seemed to him that a felt a slight, upward draught, as though a portion of the air found vent in that direction. When he mentioned it to Ariel she admitted that she had noticed the same thing, and urged him to investigate.

Leaving his Winchester with her, he began a cautious ascent

of the rugged stairs. He had about twenty feet to climb, and the greatest care was necessary. Not until at the very top, did he pass from the sight of the maiden who was attentively watching his movements.

Five minutes later, he let go his hold and dropped, down beside her. His face was flushed and his eyes glowing with excitement.

"Thank heaven!" he exclaimed, greatly agitated; "there is an opening by which we can reach the outer world."

"I was sure of it," she replied with a happy smile.

During his brief absence, she had bandaged her arm as best she could by tearing a slip from her dress. The wound bled less than would be supposed, and caused her little pain.

Taking her other hand, Ashman began helping her up among the rocks and bowlders. She needed little aid, however, for she was lighter and more graceful on her feet than he.

Sure enough, when they arrived at the top, they came upon a broader opening than that by which they had entered the cavern. It was hidden from sight by a projecting table of rock, and when they came to pass through, the outer opening was seen to be so covered by bushes that it never could have been found except by the accident which first showed Ariel the way into the cavern.

But with hearts overflowing with gratitude to heaven, they found themselves on the earth again, with the sun shining and the pure air of heaven fanning their fevered faces.

They had emerged at the crest of the mountainous mass, which covered a portion of the enchanted lake and the cavern of diamonds. Fortunately, too, they were among the woods, where they could not see far in any direction. This rendered them less liable to discovery by their enemies in the neighborhood.

Ashman held his position until the two could study their location and gain an idea of the points of the compass. The rising sun helped them to do this, and, by moving carefully about until they gained sight of the lake and the Upper Xingu, they soon ascertained in what direction the Murhapa village lay, and the course necessary to take in order to avoid it.

It was decided to put back in the forest and thread their way through the dense wilderness, striking the Xingu at a point below the rapids. There, if they found nothing of their friends, they would manage to secure a boat in which they could press their flight in the direction of the Amazon.

The forests abounded with wild animals and huge serpents, but the ardent lover was admirably armed and confident that he could protect his beloved from all harm, provided they could escape discovery by the Murhapas and Aryks.

If Haffgo should venture on an approach to the rocks, where the fugitives made their stand, he could not fail to find out the extraordinary manner in which they had eluded him, and he would be certain to organize instant pursuit.

But this was not likely to take place for a considerable time, though the possibility led Ashman to push forward with all vigor, often pausing to listen for sounds of pursuit.

The extreme caution of the lovers led them to trend much further into the woods than was really necessary, and they were a long time, therefore, in reaching the Xingu.

Edward S. Ellis

Neither had eaten food for an unusual while, but they cared nothing for that. They were too anxious for any thought except that of getting forward as fast as possible.

As they progressed, startled now and then by the prowling wild beasts which threatened attack more than once, and by the sight of enormous serpents, some in trees and some on the ground, Fred Ashman's thoughts naturally went forward, and he speculated as to what was the result of the attack on his friends the preceding night in the village.

He could comprehend the frightful situation in which they were placed by the enmity of the king, and it seemed incredible that any, or at least all of them, could have extricated themselves from their peril. Gladly would he have risked everything in their defence, but, as has been shown, that was beyond his power at any time.

The young American shrank from firing his gun, through fear of the report reaching the ears of the Murhapas. If that should take place, it would be sure to excite their suspicions, and prompt an investigation which the fugitives dreaded.

Once a jaguar became so threatening, that he leveled his weapon convinced that he must fire or be attacked, but the snarling beast finally withdrew, after sneaking behind them for a long distance.

The sun had passed the meridian when the wanderers caught the gleam of water among the trees in front. They hastened forward, and a moment's survey of the stream convinced them that they had reached the Xingu beyond all question.

Ashman recognized several features along the banks which he had noticed on his way up the river. Ariel was equally positive, so they dismissed the question from their minds.

Both were nearly exhausted, for they had had a tiresome tramp, during all of which they were under a severe mental strain. They felt that, at last, they could sit down and rest themselves before resuming their journey.

"The next thing to be done," said Ashman as he imprisoned the hand of Ariel and drew her head upon his shoulder, "is to find some boat in which we can float down stream. It will be less work than we had in ascending it."

"I suppose," she replied, "that there are people all the way along the river until you reach the end of it."

"There are; but we found most of them unfriendly long before we struck the region of the Aryks."

"Are they likely to attack us?" she asked, raising her head and looking at her lover with an alarmed expression.

"We had little difficulty, so long as we kept in the middle of the stream, and one discharge from our guns was generally enough to drive them away."

"And for how far does this prevail?"

"Two or three days ought to take us out of the danger. Then it will be plain sailing all the rest of the way. The river is long, but, dearest, we shall be with each other, and it will seem brief."

She parted her lips to make a suitable reply, when a startled expression came upon her lovely countenance and she whispered:

"They must have followed us through the woods."

Edward S. Ellis

"What do you mean?" he asked, grasping his rifle.

"I hear some one moving behind us."

"It is a wild animal—"

He checked himself, for, to his unspeakable amazement, Professor Grimcke at that instant stepped to view.

The two men caught sight of each other at the same moment. They stared as if in doubt, and then, with exclamations of delight, clasped hands.

By great good fortune, the lovers had emerged from the forest within a stone's throw of the point where Grimcke, Long, Bippo, and Pedros were waiting with the canoe hidden among the trees.

After this reunion they set out for home.

A few days carried them beyond danger, and in good time the Amazon was reached. Bippo and Pedros were left at Marcapa, at which port the explorers secured passage for home, where they arrived in safety. And in that land, so strange to the beauteous Ariel, daughter of Haffgo, king of the Murhapas, we bid good-by to our friends. But to her, Ashman was all the world; and in the sunshine of their mutual love they dwell to-day, happy, grateful, contented, and envying no one, assured, as they are, that none can be more blessed than they.

Choose from Thousands of 1stWorldLibrary Classics By

A. M. Barnard
Ada Leverson
Adolphus William Ward
Aesop
Agatha Christie
Alexander Aaronsohn
Alexander Kielland
Alexandre Dumas
Alfred Gatty
Alfred Ollivant
Alice Duer Miller
Alice Turner Curtis
Alice Dunbar
Allen Chapman
Alleyne Ireland
Ambrose Bierce
Amelia E. Barr
Amory H. Bradford
Andrew Lang
Andrew McFarland Davis
Andy Adams
Angela Brazil
Anna Alice Chapin
Anna Sewell
Annie Besant
Annie Hamilton Donnell
Annie Payson Call
Annie Roe Carr
Annonaymous
Anton Chekhov
Archibald Lee Fletcher
Arnold Bennett
Arthur C. Benson
Arthur Conan Doyle
Arthur M. Winfield
Arthur Ransome
Arthur Schnitzler
Arthur Train
Atticus
B.H. Baden-Powell
B. M. Bower
B. C. Chatterjee
Baroness Emmuska Orczy
Baroness Orczy
Basil King
Bayard Taylor
Ben Macomber
Bertha Muzzy Bower
Bjornstjerne Bjornson

Booth Tarkington
Boyd Cable
Bram Stoker
C. Collodi
C. E. Orr
C. M. Ingleby
Carolyn Wells
Catherine Parr Traill
Charles A. Eastman
Charles Amory Beach
Charles Dickens
Charles Dudley Warner
Charles Farrar Browne
Charles Ives
Charles Kingsley
Charles Klein
Charles Hanson Towne
Charles Lathrop Pack
Charles Romyn Dake
Charles Whibley
Charles Willing Beale
Charlotte M. Braeme
Charlotte M. Yonge
Charlotte Perkins Stetson
Clair W. Hayes
Clarence Day Jr.
Clarence E. Mulford
Clemence Housman
Confucius
Coningsby Dawson
Cornelis DeWitt Wilcox
Cyril Burleigh
D. H. Lawrence
Daniel Defoe
David Garnett
Dinah Craik
Don Carlos Janes
Donald Keyhoe
Dorothy Kilner
Dougan Clark
Douglas Fairbanks
E. Nesbit
E. P. Roe
E. Phillips Oppenheim
E. S. Brooks
Earl Barnes
Edgar Rice Burroughs
Edith Van Dyne
Edith Wharton

Edward Everett Hale
Edward J. O'Biren
Edward S. Ellis
Edwin L. Arnold
Eleanor Atkins
Eleanor Hallowell Abbott
Eliot Gregory
Elizabeth Gaskell
Elizabeth McCracken
Elizabeth Von Arnim
Ellem Key
Emerson Hough
Emilie F. Carlen
Emily Bronte
Emily Dickinson
Enid Bagnold
Enilor Macartney Lane
Erasmus W. Jones
Ernie Howard Pie
Ethel May Dell
Ethel Turner
Ethel Watts Mumford
Eugene Sue
Eugenie Foa
Eugene Wood
Eustace Hale Ball
Evelyn Everett-green
Everard Cotes
F. H. Cheley
F. J. Cross
F. Marion Crawford
Fannie E. Newberry
Federick Austin Ogg
Ferdinand Ossendowski
Fergus Hume
Florence A. Kilpatrick
Fremont B. Deering
Francis Bacon
Francis Darwin
Frances Hodgson Burnett
Frances Parkinson Keyes
Frank Gee Patchin
Frank Harris
Frank Jewett Mather
Frank L. Packard
Frank V. Webster
Frederic Stewart Isham
Frederick Trevor Hill
Frederick Winslow Taylor

Friedrich Kerst
Friedrich Nietzsche
Fyodor Dostoyevsky
G.A. Henty
G.K. Chesterton
Gabrielle E. Jackson
Garrett P. Serviss
Gaston Leroux
George A. Warren
George Ade
Geroge Bernard Shaw
George Cary Eggleston
George Durston
George Ebers
George Eliot
George Gissing
George MacDonald
George Meredith
George Orwell
George Sylvester Viereck
George Tucker
George W. Cable
George Wharton James
Gertrude Atherton
Gordon Casserly
Grace E. King
Grace Gallatin
Grace Greenwood
Grant Allen
Guillermo A. Sherwell
Gulielma Zollinger
Gustav Flaubert
H. A. Cody
H. B. Irving
H.C. Bailey
H. G. Wells
H. H. Munro
H. Irving Hancock
H. R. Naylor
H. Rider Haggard
H. W. C. Davis
Haldeman Julius
Hall Caine
Hamilton Wright Mabie
Hans Christian Andersen
Harold Avery
Harold McGrath
Harriet Beecher Stowe
Harry Castlemon
Harry Coghill
Harry Houidini

Hayden Carruth
Helent Hunt Jackson
Helen Nicolay
Hendrik Conscience
Hendy David Thoreau
Henri Barbusse
Henrik Ibsen
Henry Adams
Henry Ford
Henry Frost
Henry James
Henry Jones Ford
Henry Seton Merriman
Henry W Longfellow
Herbert A. Giles
Herbert Carter
Herbert N. Casson
Herman Hesse
Hildegard G. Frey
Homer
Honore De Balzac
Horace B. Day
Horace Walpole
Horatio Alger Jr.
Howard Pyle
Howard R. Garis
Hugh Lofting
Hugh Walpole
Humphry Ward
Ian Maclaren
Inez Haynes Gillmore
Irving Bacheller
Isabel Cecilia Williams
Isabel Hornibrook
Israel Abrahams
Ivan Turgenev
J.G.Austin
J. Henri Fabre
J. M. Barrie
J. M. Walsh
J. Macdonald Oxley
J. R. Miller
J. S. Fletcher
J. S. Knowles
J. Storer Clouston
J. W. Duffield
Jack London
Jacob Abbott
James Allen
James Andrews
James Baldwin

James Branch Cabell
James DeMille
James Joyce
James Lane Allen
James Lane Allen
James Oliver Curwood
James Oppenheim
James Otis
James R. Driscoll
Jane Abbott
Jane Austen
Jane L. Stewart
Janet Aldridge
Jens Peter Jacobsen
Jerome K. Jerome
Jessie Graham Flower
John Buchan
John Burroughs
John Cournos
John F. Kennedy
John Gay
John Glasworthy
John Habberton
John Joy Bell
John Kendrick Bangs
John Milton
John Philip Sousa
John Taintor Foote
Jonas Lauritz Idemil Lie
Jonathan Swift
Joseph A. Altsheler
Joseph Carey
Joseph Conrad
Joseph E. Badger Jr
Joseph Hergesheimer
Joseph Jacobs
Jules Vernes
Julian Hawthrone
Julie A Lippmann
Justin Huntly McCarthy
Kakuzo Okakura
Karle Wilson Baker
Kate Chopin
Kenneth Grahame
Kenneth McGaffey
Kate Langley Bosher
Kate Langley Bosher
Katherine Cecil Thurston
Katherine Stokes
L. A. Abbot
L. T. Meade

L. Frank Baum
Latta Griswold
Laura Dent Crane
Laura Lee Hope
Laurence Housman
Lawrence Beasley
Leo Tolstoy
Leonid Andreyev
Lewis Carroll
Lewis Sperry Chafer
Lilian Bell
Lloyd Osbourne
Louis Hughes
Louis Joseph Vance
Louis Tracy
Louisa May Alcott
Lucy Fitch Perkins
Lucy Maud Montgomery
Luther Benson
Lydia Miller Middleton
Lyndon Orr
M. Corvus
M. H. Adams
Margaret E. Sangster
Margret Howth
Margaret Vandercook
Margaret W. Hungerford
Margret Penrose
Maria Edgeworth
Maria Thompson Daviess
Mariano Azuela
Marion Polk Angellotti
Mark Overton
Mark Twain
Mary Austin
Mary Catherine Crowley
Mary Cole
Mary Hastings Bradley
Mary Roberts Rinehart
Mary Rowlandson
M. Wollstonecraft Shelley
Maud Lindsay
Max Beerbohm
Myra Kelly
Nathaniel Hawthrone
Nicolo Machiavelli
O. F. Walton
Oscar Wilde

Owen Johnson
P.G. Wodehouse
Paul and Mabel Thorne
Paul G. Tomlinson
Paul Severing
Percy Brebner
Percy Keese Fitzhugh
Peter B. Kyne
Plato
Quincy Allen
R. Derby Holmes
R. L. Stevenson
R. S. Ball
Rabindranath Tagore
Rahul Alvares
Ralph Bonehill
Ralph Henry Barbour
Ralph Victor
Ralph Waldo Emmerson
Rene Descartes
Ray Cummings
Rex Beach
Rex E. Beach
Richard Harding Davis
Richard Jefferies
Richard Le Gallienne
Robert Barr
Robert Frost
Robert Gordon Anderson
Robert L. Drake
Robert Lansing
Robert Lynd
Robert Michael Ballantyne
Robert W. Chambers
Rosa Nouchette Carey
Rudyard Kipling
Saint Augustine
Samuel B. Allison
Samuel Hopkins Adams
Sarah Bernhardt
Sarah C. Hallowell
Selma Lagerlof
Sherwood Anderson
Sigmund Freud
Standish O'Grady
Stanley Weyman
Stella Benson
Stella M. Francis

Stephen Crane
Stewart Edward White
Stijn Streuvels
Swami Abhedananda
Swami Parmananda
T. S. Ackland
T. S. Arthur
The Princess Der Ling
Thomas A. Janvier
Thomas A Kempis
Thomas Anderton
Thomas Bailey Aldrich
Thomas Bulfinch
Thomas De Quincey
Thomas Dixon
Thomas H. Huxley
Thomas Hardy
Thomas More
Thornton W. Burgess
U. S. Grant
Upton Sinclair
Valentine Williams
Various Authors
Vaughan Kester
Victor Appleton
Victor G. Durham
Victoria Cross
Virginia Woolf
Wadsworth Camp
Walter Camp
Walter Scott
Washington Irving
Wilbur Lawton
Wilkie Collins
Willa Cather
Willard F. Baker
William Dean Howells
William le Queux
W. Makepeace Thackeray
William W. Walter
William Shakespeare
Winston Churchill
Yei Theodora Ozaki
Yogi Ramacharaka
Young E. Allison
Zane Grey

www.ingramcontent.com/pod-product-compliance
Lightning Source LLC
Chambersburg PA
CBHW030122180626
46812CB00002B/519